JESSICA BECK

THE DONUT MYSTERIES, BOOK 31

CRANBERRY CRIMES

Donut Mystery #31 Cranberry Crimes

First Edition: April 2017

The First Time Ever Published!

The 31st Donut Mystery.

Jessica Beck is the *New York Times* Bestselling Author of the Donut Mysteries, the Classic Diner Mysteries, the Ghost Cat Cozy Mysteries, and the Cast Iron Cooking Mysteries.

For P and E,
Always and Forever!

When Suzanne Hart is commissioned at the last minute to make donuts for a long-time customer's birthday party, she happily complies, but when the guest of honor dies before the party can even begin, Suzanne taps Grace, Jake, and even Phillip to help her solve Jasper Finney's homicide before the killer gets away with murder.

CHAPTER 1

WE NEVER EVEN GOT TO sing "Happy Birthday" to Jasper Finney.

He'd commissioned an extravagant party for himself, but little did we know that the celebration had been arranged for something deeper, and much darker, than simply marking another year of his life. I didn't realize it at the time, but Jasper had set the wheels in motion for something bad that was going to happen well before midnight struck, and much too soon, the residents of April Springs had a brand new murder to deal with.

"How's that donut, Jasper?" I asked one of my oldest customers as he tasted a cranberry baked donut coated with a silvery glaze. Jasper Finney wasn't my oldest customer because he'd been coming to Donut Hearts longer than anyone else. It was because his time on earth exceeded that of everyone else I knew. I had to say though, that Jasper looked young for his age, but that was just because his age happened to be somewhere in the early nineties.

"It's delightful," the silver-haired man said with a grin as he looked up at me. "In all of my one hundred and thirty-seven years, I've never tasted something so delicious."

"Wow, you've aged incredibly fast lately," I said, doing my best not to smile. It was tough to do, but I knew if I did, Jasper would feel slighted, and I wasn't about to do that to him. "The last time you were in here, you were a hundred and fourteen."

"You can't blame me for shaving a few years off my total," he replied with a mischievous grin. "If I tell the truth, some folks treat me as though I were actually old!"

"Hard to believe, isn't it," I said. "Can I get you anything else?"

"No, I'm all set, but there's something that I can give you."

"What's that?" I asked, wiping up a handful of crumbs from the kids who'd been sitting near him a few moments before. When he'd sat near them, I wasn't sure how Jasper would receive their presence, especially given how loud and rowdy the boys had been, but he'd seemed absolutely delighted by their proximity and their antics.

Jasper reached into his pocket and pulled out a folded envelope. It had my name scrawled across the front of it, and I marveled at the fine details of his penmanship. It had been a different era when Jasper Finney had learned to write.

I started to open it when he put an aged hand on top of mine. "Not now, Suzanne. It's for later."

"Do you mean like after I shut the donut shop down for the day?" I asked as I held the envelope in my hand, wondering what it might be.

"No, more like when I'm gone," he said.

"So, even sooner, then," I said with a grin. "Goody. I just love surprises. I've got to warn you though, if it's a love note, my husband can be a very jealous man, particularly when the competition is coming from such a worthy rival."

"I don't mean gone, Suzanne. I mean *gone*." For once, there wasn't a touch of humor in his gaze, but I still didn't get it at that point.

I laughed. "Jasper, you'll outlive us all if you have anything to say about it. After all, you've already seen a hundred and thirty-seven years."

"True, but I'm not going to make it to one thirty-eight," he said with a shrug.

Our humorous exchange had suddenly just gotten serious. "Jasper, is there something you're not telling me? What's going on?"

"Just please do as I ask," the old man said. "I don't really want to talk about it."

I was about to push him on it anyway when his grandson came in. "Jasper, you can't just take off like that without telling anyone." I had never been a fan of Ethan Finney. How that tight-cheeked fifty-year-old stick-in-the-mud could be related to his grandfather was beyond me. Ethan was portly bordering on obese, and he seemed to be constantly sweating. There was something oily about the man that I didn't like, but maybe it was just because of the way he treated his grandfather, as though he were a foolish old man incapable of taking care of himself. Lately, Ethan had been trying to take control of his grandfather's life, without much success, I was pleased to see.

From what I could see, Jasper seemed just fine taking care of himself.

"I can, and I will continue to do so," Jasper said as he gestured to the letter and made a motion telling me that I should put it away. Whatever it was, he didn't want Ethan seeing it. I shoved it into my apron pocket, wondering what was going on.

Ethan tried to take his grandfather's arm to escort him out of Donut Hearts, but Jasper wasn't having any of that. The older man stood and said, with more than a little indignation, "Put another hand on me, my dear boy, and you'll lose it. I may be old, but I'm not too feeble to put you over my knee and give you a good spanking. Do you remember those, Ethan? You certainly needed enough of them growing up."

"You're not going to spank me, Grandfather. It's not socially acceptable any more," Ethan chided him.

"There you both are," Ethan's son, Bobby Finney—a man in his early thirties—said with obvious relief as he came into the donut shop. Bobby was just beginning to go to seed, packing on a few more pounds than was strictly necessary. I wondered if every time he looked at his father, he realized that he was seeing his future unless he did something about it, and soon. "I swear, I'm going to put tracking devices on both of you. I know April Springs is a small town, but I feel like I've been searching for days."

"Hey, Bobby," I said. I'd grown up with Bobby, though he'd been a few years behind me in school. He had mostly been known for having a quick temper back then, but since he'd come back to Elkton Falls with his father, he'd seemed to start taking after his great-grandfather instead. "Care for a donut, Bobby?"

"No one's eating any donuts," Ethan said firmly. "We're leaving."

"That's where you're wrong," Jasper said as he took his seat again. "Bobby, the cranberry donuts are amazing."

"Sounds good to me. I'll try anything once," Bobby said as he joined his great-grandfather.

Ethan stood there a moment, clearly wondering how he'd lost such complete control of the situation, and then he threw his hands up into the air. "Fine. Whatever. Do as you please."

"I plan to," Jasper said with a smile.

Ethan stormed off as I served Bobby a donut. "There you go."

"Sorry about Dad. He feels as though he's responsible for the entire clan. Just wait until Aunt Phyllis gets here."

"Phyl is coming?" I asked. Bobby's aunt was one of my mother's contemporaries, and her claim to fame in our family was that my father had taken her out twice before he'd started dating my mother. With all of Momma's successes—both in business and in life—she still resented the fact that Phyllis had ever dated my dad.

"Oh, yes. My great-grandfather has called for a grand Finney conclave for his birthday. Every last sprout left from our waning family tree will be here." Bobby took a bite of the cranberry donut, and then he smiled. "It's even better than promised."

"Thanks," I said. "Is this celebration your idea, Jasper?"

"I've called a few family and friends in to celebrate my birthday," Jasper said. "I hope you and Jake can make it."

"We wouldn't miss it for the world," I said. "When should we come?"

"Tomorrow at six," Jasper said. "You know, I've been rattling around in that big old house for far too long. Even with what little is left of my kith and kin coming, there's plenty of room at my place. Would you and Jake like to stay for the night? It would mean the world to me if you'd say yes."

"I'm not sure. I'll have to speak with my husband first," I said.

"Do that." Jasper took another bite of his donut, and then he stood. "Let's go, Bobby. Your father has stewed long enough."

"I say we let him marinate a little bit longer," Bobby said, and then he took another bite of his donut.

"You know, you can always take that donut with you."

"That's my plan," he said as he slid a single dollar bill under his plate.

It would mostly cover the cost of the donut, since I'd had to go up on my prices recently, but Jasper's substantial tip more than made up for it.

Bobby noticed the ten his great-grandfather left. "I think you made a mistake there, Jasper," he said as he retrieved the bill and tried to hand it back to him.

"I know perfectly well what I'm doing," Jasper said as he winked at me. "Put it back."

"He's right, you know," I said. "It's far too much."

"What can I say? To some, I'm feeling particularly generous."

As Bobby shrugged and replaced the bill where he'd found it, Jasper continued, "I expect you out at my place tomorrow evening, Suzanne. Convince Jake to spend the night. It should be interesting, at the very least, and I could really use both of you there." As Jasper said the last bit, his gaze looked at me imploringly. Something was going on here besides a friendly party invitation. Clearly Jasper wanted both my husband and me there, and I doubted it was because of my donut-making skills. Jake was a former state police investigator, though. Could it be that Jasper was in need of my husband's services and not mine? Lately, Jake had been toying with the idea of starting his own private detective agency, but so far, it was just that, an idea. Maybe Jasper's request would give him the push he needed to put his hard-earned skills to work.

If nothing else, it might be fun seeing Jasper tease his family and friends on his birthday, no matter what year he was celebrating.

"Do you feel like going to a party tomorrow night? It's a sleepover," I told Jake with a grin as I walked through the front door of our cottage.

"You're too late with your invitation," my husband said with a grin. "Jasper just called me."

"Man, he *really* must want us to go," I said. "What did you tell him?" I was expecting my husband to decline the offer, but I was going to do my best to talk him into going. Emma, my assistant at Donut Hearts, was already set to work the day after the party—and the one after that—with her mother, Sharon, so I was as free as a bird.

"I told him that we'd be there," Jake said. "I hope you don't mind that I spoke for the both of us. If you don't want to go, I can probably still get us out of it."

"No way. I think it sounds awesome. How old do you think Jasper really is?"

"I could ask a buddy to look it up online, but then what fun would that be?" Jake asked me with a smile. He still had strong ties with the state police, though he was reluctant to use them.

"I say we go with his latest estimate. He told me this morning that he was one hundred and thirty-seven years old."

Jake laughed. "He's the only person I know who pads his age instead of shaving years off. Do you still want to go hiking this afternoon? If you're too tired to go, I understand completely."

"No, I wouldn't miss it for the world," I said. "Let me grab a quick shower, change, and then I'll be ready to go."

"You realize that there's a good chance you'll need another shower when we get back, right?" he asked me.

"Yes, but I smell like donuts right now. I'm normally fine with it, but if we're going to be in the great outdoors, I'd actually like to smell the wildflowers instead of my own hair."

"I don't know. I like the way you smell just fine," Jake protested.

"I know that. If I fried a little bacon to add to it, it would be the perfect scent, wouldn't it?"

He nodded. "You wouldn't hear me complaining."

"I'll be ready in ten minutes, so get your hiking boots on."

"Will do," he said.

After a quick shower and a change of clothes, I felt like a brand new woman. As I was drying my hair, I told my husband, "It's a beautiful day, isn't it?"

"It is at that. Suzanne, we aren't going hiking so you can walk me like some kind of a dog, are we?" He didn't look happy about the prospect.

I shook my head. "No way. I need the exercise a lot more

than you do. Try working around donuts all day long and see how long it takes for *your* jeans to get tight."

"Are you sure?" he asked me intently.

"Positive. It will be good for both of us," I said as I reached down, grabbed his hand, and pulled him up off the couch. "Come on. I'll race you to the truck. The winner gets to drive it."

He laughed. "I didn't think you liked driving my old beater."

"What can I say? It's growing on me."

We raced to the truck at full speed. I would have beat him, too, but he cut me off at the last second as he lunged for the bed of the truck and tapped it. "I win. I get to drive."

"Fine," I said. "But I almost beat you. You know that, don't you?"

"That's why I'm happy we're taking this walk."

"It's not a walk. It's a hike," I said.

"Strolling to the top of the waterfall is not what I'd call an endurance expedition," Jake replied.

"Maybe not, but it's the best hike we have around." I'd been reluctant to ever take that hike again after what had happened on it to me once, but I'd finally gotten over it, and Jake and I were now making it at least a weekly outing lately.

I'd actually lost two pounds since we'd started.

He'd lost five.

I wondered if he wasn't sneaking out and exercising while I was at work. If he was, then good for him. Hiking the trail also gave us a chance to chat without any outside distractions other than nature itself.

After we parked and started the ascent, I said, "Ethan Finney came by the donut shop and collected Jasper today as though he were a little boy playing hooky from school."

"Did Jasper make a scene?"

"No, Bobby came by before they could really get into it. When he sided with his great-grandfather, I thought Ethan was going to blow his top," I said, catching my breath as I hiked upward. The view at the top was worth it, but it took some doing to get there.

"That family appears to be a little odd," Jake said. I was miffed that he didn't seem to be out of breath at all, and my suspicion that he'd been secretly exercising without me was growing. "Did Jasper always have money?" he asked me.

"From what I understand, he was born into it, but then he multiplied it substantially running a factory just out of town. No one really knows how much he's worth, but it's got to be in the millions."

Jake whistled softly beside me. "Wow. That's a lot of money. People have been known to do some pretty bad things for a great deal less."

I stopped for a moment. "What is that supposed to mean?"

"Nothing," Jake said, brushing my question off. "I just have a suspicious mind. That's all. Put it down to what I did for a living once upon a time. Speaking of making a living, I've been thinking about something lately."

There was dead air between us for a few seconds. Honestly, I was afraid to say much of anything. I knew that my husband had been getting restless ever since he'd left the state police, but I also realized that if he was going to find a second career, he was going to have to do it on his own, without any prompting from me. "Yes?" I asked when I wasn't sure he was going to continue.

"I may take your advice after all," Jake said, as though every word cost him money.

"Wonderful! That's excellent news! Exactly *which* piece of advice are we talking about?" I asked him with a grin.

"I thought I might start conducting a few private inquiries on my own," he said. "I wouldn't take any divorce cases or custody battles."

"What does that leave?" I asked, not wanting to discourage him but also hoping that he would go into it with open eyes.

"Honest-to-goodness puzzles that need solving. What do you think?"

"I think it's a great idea," I said approvingly.

"Could that be because *you're* the one who first suggested it?" he asked as I slipped on a wet part of the path.

"Maybe, but it really doesn't matter *who* came up with the plan. I think it's exciting. You can use the building my father left me. All we need is a sign out front, some business cards, and some stationery, and you'll be in business."

"I'm afraid that it's a little more involved than that," Jake amended.

"Then we'll do whatever we need to in order to get this thing rolling."

Jake stopped, grabbed my arm, and faced me on the narrow path. "Suzanne, as much as I appreciate your enthusiasm, this project is all mine. I wouldn't dream of telling you how to run Donut Hearts, so leave this to me, okay?"

"Got it," I said lightly. I wasn't even hurt by the rebuff. I was simply thrilled that my husband was going to do something that made him feel productive again. If he'd been content with his early retirement, no one would have supported it more than I would have, but the fact was that he'd been listless and a little lost lately, and I hated seeing him like that. "Go at your own pace." I looked up the path and saw that we still had quite a ways to go before we made it to the top. "This thing feels as though it gets longer and longer every time we scale it."

"There's not much more to go," Jake said with a grin. "Come on. I'll race you to the top."

"Have you been working out in secret?" I finally asked him. There was no way I could even manage a fast climb at that point, let alone a full-on race.

"I may have taken this trail a time or two without you," he answered with a grin. "Mad?"

"Are you kidding? I'm delighted," I said as I reached out and grabbed him. After giving my husband a sound kiss, I stepped past him and hurried up the path. "Come on, slowpoke. What are you waiting for?"

Jake ended up beating me handily, but I didn't mind.

My husband had gotten his spark back, and I was absolutely delighted.

We'd be celebrating more than Jasper's birthday the next night. We would also be christening my husband's new business venture and his renewed sense of purpose in life. I'd heard that all anyone ever needed was love and work in their lives, and I believed it. Even Momma and her husband, Phillip, were extremely active—my mother with her many business and real estate ventures and Phillip with his cold case research on crimes that had happened decades before. The donut shop kept me hopping, and I had no intention of leaving it any time soon, so Jake finding a new purpose was exactly what he needed.

CHAPTER 2

"COME ON IN," TRISH SAID giddily as we entered the Boxcar Grill. "Order whatever you want. This evening, everything is on the house!"

"What's going on?" I asked my friend. Trish had certainly been generous in the past, but this was crazy. The diner was already brimming with people, and I wondered if everyone else there was enjoying free meals as well.

"I won the lottery!" Trish said jubilantly. "This is my last night running the Boxcar."

"You're shutting the place down?" I asked her. "Exactly how much did you win?"

"A cool million," she said. "A customer left me his ticket as a tip, and on a whim I checked it on the computer. It matched all of the numbers except the Powerball, which means I just made a million bucks."

"So you're quitting?" Jake asked her. "How much of that will you actually get to keep?"

"I looked it up online after I saw that it was a winner. Some guy in Rocky Mount won a million a few years ago, and he got a check for $692,000."

"Is that enough to retire on?" Jake asked.

"I figure it's going to last me just fine, with what I've got put back anyway," she said, and then she patted his shoulder.

"Thanks for worrying about me, Jake, but I'm going to be fine. I'm not going to waste my money."

"More burgers for the table, please," Betilda Enwright asked Trish loudly. "With extra fries, too."

"I thought you said you weren't going to waste any money," I told her.

"This? I'm just cleaning out our inventory."

"What about Hilda and Gladys?" I asked softly. They'd worked for Trish for years, and I hated to see them lose out because of their boss's good fortune.

"They're happy for me," Trish said with the hint of a frown on her lips, "and you should be, too."

"We are," I said quickly. "Any chance we could get burgers and fries, too?"

"You betcha," Trish said with a grin. "I'll even hold back some peanut butter pie for you, too."

"That sounds excellent," I said. We couldn't find any tables free, but then I heard someone call my name. Momma and Phillip had a table to themselves, and they motioned for us to join them.

"Did you know about this?" Jake asked them as we sat down.

"We just walked in ourselves. As a matter of fact, I was just getting ready to call you," Momma said.

"What do you think about it?" Jake asked her.

"I'm worried about Trish," Momma admitted. "It may seem like a great deal of money to her right now, but I'm not at all sure how she's going to make it last."

"That's my concern, too," Jake replied.

"Should I talk to her?" I volunteered. I would hate for a windfall to turn into a nightmare for one of my closest friends.

"Maybe it would be prudent," Momma said.

I made my way forward and found Trish speaking with a

man I didn't recognize. There was a look of shock on her face, and I wondered what was going on.

"I just don't believe it," she said.

"Believe what?" I asked her, butting in, whether it was welcome or not. That was what friends did, at least as far as I was concerned.

"He says the ticket doesn't belong to me," Trish replied, clearly on the brink of tears.

"Explain yourself," I told the man.

"It's simple, really. My client inadvertently left the ticket behind, not as a tip, but by accident. It belongs to him, and so does the million dollars."

"That's not fair," Trish said, looking as though she'd just lost her best friend.

"What is unfair is you taking something that doesn't belong to you," the attorney said curtly as he handed her a piece of paper.

"What's this?" Trish asked him numbly.

"It's an injunction not to do anything with that ticket until the court can resolve its true ownership. There is a hearing in two days, and I suggest you find representation of your own. Good evening."

After he was gone, Trish looked at me, clearly stunned by the news. "What am I going to do?"

"You're going to fight it, naturally," I said. "But first things first. We need to stop this free-for-all ordering spree."

"I don't have the heart to do it," Trish said.

"No worries. I'll do it for you." I turned to the raucous crowd and said, "May I have your attention, please? Everyone, settle down."

No one listened until my mother stood and said, "Quiet!"

Though she was an older, petite woman, there was nothing small about her voice.

The room hushed immediately.

I nodded my thanks, and then I made my announcement. "Apparently there is some dispute about the true ownership of Trish's ticket. Until it can be resolved, I'm afraid that no one's eating for free tonight."

"But she already offered us free food," Belinda complained.

"You can't take something like that back," Wally Strong chimed in from a different table. "It's got to be against the law. It's bait and switch, or at least something like that."

Things were quickly getting out of hand.

Trish touched my shoulder, and then she said softly, "It's fine, Suzanne."

"No, it's not," I replied.

In a louder voice, she faced her diners and said, "Folks, if you're going to take advantage of my generosity, then go right ahead. I won't charge anyone for their meals. After all, a promise is a promise."

There was a loud cheer until she held up a hand and continued, "But if I *don't* get the winnings, then my prices are going to have to go up to cover my losses tonight."

"Tell you what, everybody," I said. "Don't pay your bills, but I urge you all to leave tips large enough to make it worth Trish's while to stay in business if things don't work out. In the meantime, any future free food offer has been rescinded as of right now. Anyone who has a problem with that can take it up with me up front."

There was some grumbling from the crowd, but nobody directly challenged me.

"Thanks, Suzanne," Trish said softly. The poor thing looked as though she were about to completely lose it, and I couldn't blame her.

"Don't worry. We'll figure something out," I said, doing my best to reassure her. "We would still like our food, but we're paying full price, of course. Okay?"

"No," she said firmly. "You made your orders when you thought it was going to be free. I won't go back on my word."

"Then we'll just over-tip you," I said with a grin. "Trish, you know you can't out-stubborn me, don't you?"

The diner owner laughed softly. "It would take too much effort at this point to even try. What a mess."

"Not to pile on, but I have a hunch that it's only going to get messier from here," I said.

"Thanks for the words of encouragement," she said.

Belinda and her party stood and moved toward the door. "You can cancel our orders for extra burgers and fries," she said as she tried to make her way out without leaving a cent behind.

"Aren't you forgetting something, Belinda?" I asked her.

"Don't worry. We left a tip at the table."

"Fine. I'll go collect it, and then I'll clean the table for Trish myself," I said sternly. "I think we should announce all of the customers' generosity to everyone else, don't you?"

"Oh, all right," she said as she dove into her purse, pulled out a twenty, and shoved it into my hand. "Happy?"

"No, but I'm getting there," I said with a smile. "You have a nice night now, you hear?"

"I will," she said, her voice dripping with sarcasm.

Once Belinda and her party were gone, Trish grinned in spite of her dire mood. "You're a wicked woman, Suzanne Hart. You know that, don't you?"

"As a matter of fact, I take great pride in it," I said as I gave her the twenty. "Let me go grab the rest of your tip for you."

"I can do that myself," she said.

"But then I wouldn't have the satisfaction of seeing how much Belinda was planning to leave you before I stepped in," I said as I grabbed a plastic tub and moved to clear the table in question.

After I finished cleaning away the dishes, I found a five and three singles left behind. Even with the twenty, it would barely cover the table's tab, based on the plates I'd removed. Oh, well. I was sure that some folks would over-tip before they left.

"Are we working for our meal tonight?" Phillip asked when I returned to the table. "I've always wanted to run one of those commercial dishwashers. Do you think she'd let me have a turn at it?"

"Be careful what you wish for," Jake said. "I ran one during a summer spent at camp, and the thing nearly scalded me alive on more than one occasion. We named the thing 'the Beast,' and with good reason, too."

"Okay, you've convinced me," Phillip said, clearly rethinking his previous offer. "Maybe I'll just leave a good tip instead."

"We all will," Momma said as she patted her husband's arm. My mother stared worriedly at Trish, who looked absolutely lost. "I'm concerned about her, Suzanne."

"She'll be okay," I said, "but if you know any good lawyers, I'd appreciate it if you'd steer one her way."

"I can do better than that," Momma said. "A certain barrister in Charlotte owes me a personal favor. He doesn't know it yet, but he's about to take on her case, pro bono."

"I've known a few lawyers in my life, but I haven't seen one yet willing to work for free without some kind of reason," Phillip said.

"Oh, he has reason enough," Momma said smugly.

"But you're not going to tell us what it is, are you?" he asked his wife.

Momma just smiled. "Phillip, there have to be *some* secrets between us. That's what helps keep life interesting."

"Speaking of interesting, you'll never believe what happened at the donut shop today," I said, trying to shift the focus away from Trish's woes.

"Jasper Finney invited you to his birthday party sleepover," Momma said.

"How could you have possibly known that?" I asked her. My mother often surprised me, but I was stunned that she knew about the happenings in Donut Hearts so quickly.

"It's simple, really. He invited us, too," Momma said.

"Are you going?" Jake asked her.

"We wouldn't miss it for the world," she said with clear delight. "Jasper was particularly intent on having Phillip attend."

"Why he would request my presence is beyond me," the former police chief said. "We've never really been all that close."

"Funny, but he was insistent that Jake come as well," I said. "I wonder if he thinks there's a reason to invite two former police chiefs to his soiree."

"I don't know, but why don't you find out?" Jake asked me.

"What did you have in mind?"

"It's easy enough. Call Grace and see if she and Chief Grant have been invited, too," my husband suggested.

It only took a quick phone call to confirm that Jake's hunch had been right.

"Wow, that's a lot of lawmen gathered together for one night, isn't it?" Momma asked after I got off the phone with Grace.

"*Something's* going on," I said. "I just don't know what it is yet." I wasn't ready to share Jasper's conversation with me about his impending demise, or at least the implication of it.

"Well, we'll find out soon enough," Phillip said. "After all, the party is tomorrow evening."

"I'm not sure I'm going to be able to wait until then," I said. "After I close the donut shop tomorrow, I'm going to go speak with Jasper and see if I can find out what's really going on."

"You'll have to do it without me," Jake said. "I've got that thing in Hickory over the next few days, remember?" He was consulting with the police there on a case, something that had been arranged well before we'd learned of Jasper's party.

"Just be back in time for the festivities," I said.

"It shouldn't take long, but I don't want you going out there by yourself, just in case."

"We could always cancel *our* plans and go with you," Momma suggested. "We were going to look at some investment property in Boone tomorrow, but it can wait."

"No, you go ahead. I'm sure Grace will go with me."

"If she can't make it, call us," Phillip said.

"Will do."

"Why don't you call her right now?" Momma suggested.

"Fine." I dialed my best friend's number, and Grace picked up on the second ring.

"Wow, two phone calls in less than an hour. Do you miss me that much, Suzanne? I know it's been a few days since we've hung out, but you're getting kind of needy, aren't you?" Her laughter confirmed that she was just teasing me.

"Do you have any plans tomorrow after lunch? I thought I'd pop in on Jasper and see what's really going on with this party of his."

"It just so happens that I'm free," she said. "I just got a text from Mindy White. Things must be crazy at the Boxcar with Trish giving away the store. I'll be over there in a minute myself."

"She isn't sure she'll get to keep the winnings, so the free-food frenzy is off," I explained.

"Then there's no reason for me to rush over there, is there?" Grace asked me.

"You make a good living. Do you really need a free meal?" I asked her.

"Need? No, of course not. Want? That's something else entirely. What happened with Trish's ticket?"

"It's a long story, so I'll tell you tomorrow," I said as I saw the diner owner approaching with our food order.

"Until then," Grace said, and I put my phone away.

After we ate, the place had cleared out considerably. Trish was still overwhelmed with the piles of dirty dishes everywhere, so we all pitched in and cleared the rest of the tables for her, carrying the now-full bins to the front.

"Where should we put these?" Jake offered.

"That table will be fine," she said. "I think I'm going to close early. Tonight has been a lot to process."

"I bet," I said as I handed her the sizeable tips we'd collected from the tables we'd cleared. "How much of a hit are you going to take because of this?"

"Wait. Here's ours, too," Momma said as she shoved more money at Trish.

"This is too much, Dot," Trish protested.

"Nonsense," Momma said. "You earned every penny of it."

I noticed that Trish didn't protest too much. As she counted the cash in her hand and rang it into the register, she looked at us in wonder. "Actually, I made more than I would have if I'd charged everyone full price and still took in their tips," she said. "Maybe that should be my new policy. No charge for food, but tip whatever you want."

"I believe tonight was a special circumstance," Momma said.

"I know. I was just teasing. Thanks again. For everything."

"Oh, we're not finished yet," Momma said. "Don't worry about legal representation. I have an excellent attorney in Charlotte who is going to be more than happy to represent you."

"I'm not sure I can afford an excellent attorney," Trish said with a wry grin. "I was kind of hoping for one that was barely competent, and that's still going to be a stretch."

"No worries about his fee. He owes me a favor, and I mean to collect."

"On my behalf?" Trish asked. "Dot, I couldn't accept that from you."

"I'm afraid you have no choice," Momma said as she kissed

Trish's cheek. "You've been such a good friend to my daughter over the years that you feel as though you are one of my own."

"Hearing that is actually nicer than getting a free lawyer," Trish said, looking as though she was fighting back tears yet again.

"Let's get out of here before she has a well-deserved meltdown," I suggested. After the others filed out, I hugged her as I added, "We're here if you need us."

"I can't tell you how much that means to me," she said.

"Hey, you heard Momma. You're like family to us, and we'd do anything for our own," I said. "Try to get some sleep tonight, okay?"

"I'll try, but I'm not making any promises."

I found Jake outside waiting for me, though Momma and Phillip had already gone. "Suzanne, I could cancel my thing in Hickory tomorrow if you'd like me to."

"You go on. Grace and I have this covered, but don't forget, I want you back in time for the party."

"There's no way I'm missing that," he said. "Shall we head home?"

I stifled a yawn as I agreed. "Sounds like a solid plan to me. I'm beat, and it will be time to make the donuts again soon enough."

Truer words were never spoken. I loved my job, but sometimes it got a little tiring doing the same thing day in and day out.

But then again, I was grateful for something valuable to do with my time, and I was overjoyed that soon enough, Jake would have something in his life as well.

CHAPTER 3

"SUZANNE HART, PLEASE," A WOMAN'S voice requested when I answered the phone at Donut Hearts the next morning. The entire town had been buzzing about Jasper's party. Many of them had been invited to the festivities, though only a select few were included in the sleepover afterward.

"This is Suzanne," I told her, and then, as I handed Nick Williams his change, I said, "Thanks."

"I don't understand. Why are you thanking me?" she asked me.

"I wasn't. I was waiting on a customer. Don't worry, I can multitask. Now, what can I do for you?"

There was a long pause, and then the woman asked, "Are you talking to me now?"

"I am," I said, wondering how I'd gotten onto this particular conversational merry-go-round.

"My name is Bethesda Long. I'm coordinating the festivities for the Finney party tonight." I'd heard of Bethesda. She was Union Square's preeminent party planner, and from what I understood, she charged a premium for her services. Leave it to Jasper to go all out for his hundred and thirty-seventh birthday party.

"Congratulations," I said. "Was that all you needed to talk to me about?" I asked her as another customer approached. "What can I do for you today?"

"That's what I'm trying to get to," Bethesda said, clearly growing as impatient with our conversation as I was.

"Not you," I said.

The customer looked at me with raised eyebrows.

"You," I told him as I pointed in his direction.

"Well, which is it?" she asked, clearly frustrated.

"Bethesda, call me back in two minutes. I'll get my assistant up front and we can speak uninterrupted."

"I don't have two minutes," she said stiffly.

"Then I suppose we're finished," I replied. "Thanks for calling. Bye now."

After I hung up, I told the man, "My apologies. I had someone on the phone who just wouldn't get to the point. Now, what can I get for you?"

"Coffee, black, old-fashioned donut, one."

Wow, that was succinct. I filled his order, took his money and made change, and then I called out to Emma in the kitchen. "Got a second?"

"Sure thing, boss."

"Take the front. There's a phone call that I'm about to have to answer."

Emma looked at me, puzzled. "Suzanne, how could you possibly know that?"

At that moment, my cell phone rang. I grinned at her as I explained, "Who knows? Maybe I'm psychic."

"Maybe you are," Emma said as she moved out of the kitchen out to the front.

"Thanks for calling me back," I said as I answered my phone. I'd glanced at the caller ID, and I'd recognized the number from earlier.

"Will we be disturbed again?" Bethesda asked.

"I don't think so, but I'd still advise you to make it dance, just in case."

"Very well. I'll get to the point. The baker supplying tonight's birthday cake has canceled on me at the last minute."

"I'm sorry, but what does that have to do with me? I bake a fair cake, but my mother makes the best ones in the family. Ask anybody."

"Unfortunately, there has been a change in Mr. Finney's request. Instead of cake, the guest of honor would now like eighteen dozen donuts instead. He's willing to pay a premium for his request, but I assured him that there was no way you could supply such an expansive order on such short notice. I'm afraid he was rather insistent though, so if you'll just tell me no, and I can relay the information to him for you and move on to one of my other contingency plans."

"I can do that," I said. Fortunately, we'd just gotten a fresh shipment of supplies delivered, and I had everything on hand that I'd need.

"Good," she said, clearly relieved. "I'll give Mr. Finney your regrets."

"Hang on. You didn't understand. I want to make them for him. After all, how many one hundred and thirty-seventh birthday parties do most people get?"

"Surely you don't have time for that," she said.

"As a matter of fact, I have *more* than enough time." I'd wanted to see Jasper anyway, but this was the perfect opportunity to finagle an invitation before everyone else arrived. "I'll just need to go over a few details with you in person, and then I can get started."

"I'm afraid I'm not going to be able to leave the residence today," she said firmly.

That was what I'd been counting on. "I suppose I can make my way out there." I glanced at the clock. "In fact, I can be there in half an hour."

"I understand. I can write you a check for the deposit

when you arrive, with the balance delivered upon the receipt of donuts."

Did she honestly think I was refusing to work for one of my favorite customers without getting partial payment up front first? The woman clearly misread me, but since it worked in my favor, I decided not to correct her. "Good. Then we're on the same page." I had a burst of inspiration as I added, "I have a temporary catering aide I'll be bringing with me as well." I just hoped Grace was off work already and that she could come with me.

"Very well. I'll see you both shortly."

"Bye, and thanks for calling," I replied.

"I'm afraid that Mr. Finney would have it no other way," she said. I knew firsthand how stubborn the older man could be.

In fact, it was a common trait we shared.

I walked back out front and saw that we had less than ten minutes left in our workday, even though it was just ten till eleven in the morning. It made sense in the donut-making world, though, since I'd started my shift at three a.m.

"Do you have any plans this afternoon?" I asked Emma. "You don't have class today, do you?"

"No, I'm off. As a matter of fact, I thought about going shopping in Hudson Creek," she said.

"How would you like to make enough money to make that trip a lot more fun tomorrow?" I asked her.

"I'm intrigued. What's up?" Emma asked me.

"We just got a surprise order for eighteen dozen donuts for Jasper Finney's party this evening, and they're paying us handsomely for the privilege. Instead of your normal wages, I'll give you time and a half, or we can split the profits down the middle after we take out our expenses. It's your call."

"I'll take the profit split," she said with a grin nearly before I could finish making my offer.

"You don't even need to think about it first?" I asked her, smiling at my donut shop protégé.

"No, ma'am. I haven't been taking business courses for nothing."

"Good. That's what I was about to suggest anyway. We should both make out just fine, given what they're paying us."

"Then let's make some donuts," Emma said with more enthusiasm than even I could muster. Then again, I had quite a few years on her. I'd been young and full of energy once upon a time, but that was before I'd started running Donut Hearts.

"Slow down, girl. We've got some time before we need to get started, and I need to run out to Jasper's place first. Do you mind finishing up here, making out the deposit, and dropping it off at the bank while I'm doing that?"

"No worries. I've got it under control. Should I call Mom in to help out, too?"

"Do we really need her?" I asked.

"No. Of course not. I was just trying to share the wealth, that's all," Emma admitted.

"You know what? It might be fun to have her working with us. Go ahead and invite her. We can split the profits into thirds, and we'll all make out," I said.

Emma frowned for a moment before speaking. "I didn't mean it that way, Suzanne. I'll split my half with her. You deserve half all to yourself."

I didn't feel like getting into an argument about it with her. "First call her and see if she's free. *Then* we'll discuss the cash disbursement arrangement."

Emma nodded. After a quick phone conversation, she said, "It doesn't matter. Mom's tied up."

"Then our problem is solved. It was nice of you to offer, though."

My assistant shrugged. "The older I get, the more I realize I won't have my folks around forever. It really makes you appreciate them, doesn't it?"

I'd lost my own father several years earlier, and if anything, I'd grown closer to my mother than we'd ever been in the years since, even moving back in with her after my divorce. "I get it. You could always buy her something special with part of your share."

"That's a great idea," Emma said. "Now shoo. You have a meeting to get to."

"Let me call Grace first," I said.

"Call her as you drive over there," Emma insisted. "I don't want you jeopardizing our extra income." Her smile told me that she was only partially teasing.

Fortunately, Grace was home, which I found out after a twenty-second drive down Springs Drive to her place. If I'd had five more seconds, I could have made it all the way home, but I wasn't heading there, at least not just yet.

"Feel like taking a road trip with me?" I asked Grace over the phone as I sat in her driveway in my Jeep.

"You know it. Swing by and pick me up." That was one thing I loved about Grace. She didn't need to know the details. All I had to do was make the offer, no matter what it was, and she was in.

"I was hoping you'd say that. Look out the window. I'm in your driveway."

"Cool. Okay, I'll be out in a second," Grace said, and she was nearly as good as her word. My best friend had changed from the fancy suit she'd no doubt worn to work into casual slacks and a blouse. The funny thing was that her leisure attire was always nicer than my fanciest outfits. I just seemed to feel most comfortable in blue jeans and T-shirts, while she fit in perfectly in the corporate world and the glamour of her position in a cosmetics company.

As Grace got into the passenger side of the Jeep, she asked me, "Where are we going?"

"I'm supplying the donuts for Jasper's party tonight, so I need to run out to his place to clear a few things up first," I said as I pulled out of her driveway and started toward the Finney estate.

"Why didn't you mention that when we spoke last night?" she asked me.

"Mainly because I just found out myself," I admitted.

"Correct me if I'm wrong, but if that's the case, shouldn't you be making donuts right about now instead of running around town with me?"

"Don't worry. We have time to do both," I said.

"*We?* You don't think I'm helping you produce the order, do you?" Grace asked, clearly appalled by the possibility.

"Not 'you and me' we, 'Emma and me' we," I explained.

"That's a convoluted sentence, even for you, Suzanne. So, if you two are making donuts, why are we going out to Jasper's place?"

"I made up an excuse, but the truth is, I'm worried about him," I explained. "If I wait to speak with him tonight at the party, I'll never get him alone. Jasper's been acting odd lately."

"How could you tell?" Grace asked, and then she quickly added, "I didn't mean that the way it must have sounded. It's just that Jasper Finney has always danced to the beat of his own drum."

"Isn't that marched?" I asked her.

"March, dance, it's all the same to me. He's an odd bird," Grace answered.

"Remind me never to go dancing with you. Or marching either, for that matter," I said with a smile.

"The question is," Grace said, "what makes Jasper's actions remarkable at the moment?"

"Well, for one thing, he gave me a letter yesterday," I admitted.

"He mailed it, you mean," Grace tried to correct me.

"No, I chose my words carefully. He was at the donut shop yesterday, and he handed it to me."

"What did it say?" Grace asked.

"I don't know," I admitted.

I glanced over as I was driving and saw that my best friend was frowning in my direction. "Let me get this straight. Jasper handed you a letter yesterday, but you haven't opened it yet so you could read it. Are you sure *he's* the one that's been acting a bit off lately? Maybe the donut fumes are finally getting to you."

"There's no doubt about it, but I didn't read it for a perfectly valid reason," I explained.

"Why not? Was it in French? You were never really very good at the language in high school," Grace said before I could go into any more detail.

"Why would it be in French?" I asked her, honestly curious about how her mind was working at the moment.

"I don't have any idea," Grace said. "It's your story."

"So how about letting me tell it, then?" I asked her, doing my best not to shake my head in disbelief. I wasn't sure if she was joking with me or if she was honestly having trouble following our conversation, but we didn't have a great deal of time before we arrived.

"Go on. I'm listening," Grace answered, and as I looked over at her quickly again, I saw her wink in my direction.

Good. She'd just been pulling my leg after all.

"He asked me not to read it until he was dead," I explained.

"I'm sorry," Grace said, her voice full of contrition.

"Why?"

"I thought we were just goofing around. I didn't know Jasper was dying," she said.

"He's not, at least not any more quickly than the rest of us," I amended.

"It's an odd request then, isn't it?" Grace asked. "Are you telling me that you weren't even tempted to peek at it?"

"I was tempted, all right," I admitted.

"But you didn't give in to the temptation."

"No, at least not yet. I still need to speak with him, though."

Before we had time for any more conversation, we were there. As I drove the Jeep down the long driveway to the two-story brick colonial, I saw trucks, rental vans, outdoor activity tents, and a host of what must have been vehicles the temporary workers had arrived in.

"Wow. This is going to be some party," Grace said beside me as I found a spot and wedged my Jeep into it. That was one of the joys of driving such a small vehicle; I could park it just about anywhere.

"I'm not really all that surprised, knowing Jasper," I said. "Are you?"

"The levels of my astonishment are hard to quantify when it comes to men in general," Grace said. "Let's go in and see if we can locate Jasper."

"First we need to find Bethesda Long. Once that's settled, then we can go looking for Jasper," I explained.

"Then by all means, let's go find the Party Queen," Grace said, and we headed inside.

CHAPTER 4

"Wow, I've never been here before, have you?" Grace asked me as we walked in through the open door and started looking around.

"It looks more like a movie set than an actual home," I said, whispering without knowing why. From the gleaming highly polished floors to the coffered ceilings resplendent with crown molding, it was a true showplace. I looked around at the furniture and realized that everything I was looking at was an antique. The hall table alone was probably worth more than my Jeep had been when it was brand new. The staircase leading up was made from marble, and the chandelier in the entryway had so much crystal in it that if the light hit just right, it would be blinding.

"A busy movie set at that," Grace said as she suddenly ducked out of the way. A troop of folks were bringing in folding tables, no doubt set for the feast. As big as the place was, it still felt as though we were in the way.

"Suzanne Hart, Grace Gauge, what are you two doing here?" a familiar voice asked me from behind.

I turned to find Angelica DeAngelis standing there, the matriarch and owner of Napoli's, my favorite Italian restaurant in the world, located in a strip mall in nearby Union Square. Angelica was a true Italian beauty, and though her daughters were each lovely in their own right, none of them could hold a candle to their mother's allure.

"I'm providing dessert," I said as I hugged her before she moved on to Grace. "How about you?"

"I'm supplying the main courses," she said. "I hope you're further along with your prep work than I am with mine."

"If you're here, then who's running the restaurant?" I asked her.

"Sophia is working with me. Maria and Antonia are handling things at Napoli's without us, and Tianna even agreed to pitch in." Tianna, Angelica's oldest daughter, was back in the fold after a long estrangement. It was good to see how happy the reconciliation had made my friend. She smiled as she added, "I'd love to chat, but I'm needed in the kitchen. Talk to you soon."

With that, Angelica was gone.

"Mrs. Hart, I presume?" a small, birdlike woman asked me from the corridor as she clutched a clipboard as though it were a life preserver and she was at sea. "I'm Bethesda Long."

"Suzanne works just fine," I said as I offered my hand. "This is Grace."

Bethesda didn't take my hand, simply nodding instead. The poor woman looked as though she had been strained to the breaking point, and I felt bad for insisting on our meeting, though I had no real desire to speak with her. Grace and I were there for Jasper and Jasper alone. "Thank you for stepping in at the last second. When I told Mr. Finney, he seemed delighted by the news. In fact, he insisted that I pay you in full upon your arrival, though that's generally not my policy at all."

"I'd be happy to wait," I said, ignoring the check she began waving at me as though it were an extinguisher and I was on fire.

"Nonsense. As I said, Mr. Finney demanded that it be handled this way."

"Have you known him long?" I asked her.

"Ages, in fact. My father used to work for him in the factory, so you can imagine my delight when he called to ask me to plan this celebration."

I took the check, quickly glancing at the amount. As I tried to hand it back to her, I said, "I'm sorry, but you've made a mistake."

"I can assure you, that doesn't happen," Bethesda Long said primly.

"The thing is, it's made out for far too much," I insisted. "See for yourself."

The party planner studied the check for a moment, and then she nodded. "The total is correct. It includes additional funds due to the last-minute nature of the request. Please take it. I don't have time to issue you another one, and I have no desire to convey your refusal to my employer."

I thought about fighting her on it, but she was right. It wasn't her problem to handle, but now I had something else I needed to discuss with Jasper Finney. "Thanks are in order, then, I suppose," I said.

"You're very welcome, but it's Mr. Finney you should be thanking. Now, is there anything else I can do for you? I hate to be so abrupt, but I really am pushed for time."

"No, we're good," I said, and she nodded as she hurried away in Angelica's general direction.

"What was that all about?" Grace asked me. "Did they really pay you too much?"

"It's not permanent," I assured her. "That's just one more thing I need to take up with Jasper now."

"I wouldn't do that if I were you," Grace said so softly that I nearly missed it.

"What do you mean?"

"You heard the woman. Jasper insisted on doing it. Think about how he's going to take it if you refuse his generosity,"

Grace explained. "You know him better than I do, but if I had to describe him, I'd say that he was quirky, and also full of pride."

"Okay," I said reluctantly. "You know, I hate when you do that."

"Do what?" she asked, clearly made curious by my statement.

"Be right," I said. I decided not to push the payment issue after all, since I had something far more serious I wanted to discuss with the birthday host. "Where should we start looking for him?"

Grace looked around the house, at least the parts of it that we could see from our vantage point. "I don't have a clue."

"Let's try upstairs," I suggested. After all, that might serve to get us out of the way of the temporary workers, since the entry was teeming with people moving in and out of the structure as though they were ants.

"I'm game if you are. If we're going to get caught wandering around, it might as well be with good reason."

When we got to the top of the stairs and close to the first door—which just happened to be ajar—I paused for a moment. After lifting a finger to my lips, I motioned to the opening and tried to hear what was being said inside.

"I'm telling you, it's not right," Bobby Finney said. "We can't do it. *I* can't do it."

"We can, and we will," Ethan, his father said. Their voices were distinct enough to hear every word, and identifying them was simplicity itself. "Robert, it has to be done."

"Then do it without me," Bobby said, and then I heard angry footsteps approaching us. Jasper's great-grandson was leaving! Grabbing Grace's arm, I pulled her forward, not back down the stairs we'd just traversed. I knew if we did that, there might be some suspicion that we'd fled upon hearing their plans. It would have been true enough, but I didn't want it to seem that way.

The hallway was lined with paintings, and as the door was

flung open, I peered at the closest portrait, trying desperately to decipher the artists' name. "I told you it wasn't a Vermeer," I said, not having a clue if it was or not. I'd seen a public television show on classical artists, and just as I'd been nodding off, I'd heard the name, and it had stuck.

"Of course it's not a Vermeer," Bobby said. "Not only is it the wrong style, but you're off by two and a half centuries."

Ethan soon joined us. "What's going on?"

Before I could come up with an excuse, Bobby said, "They were wondering who painted the portrait."

"Who cares?" Ethan asked. "Why are you two here?"

Grace was about to answer with what would have no doubt been an entertaining story, but I decided to provide the truth instead. "I'm providing dessert for the festivities tonight."

"Yes, I heard about that," Ethan said, clearly displeased by the prospect.

"Personally, I think it's a great idea," Bobby said, beaming.

"You would," the man's father said. "Ladies, I'm sure you need to get started on those donuts right away, so don't let us keep you."

The way he stood there staring at us, I realized that there was no way we'd ever be able to search for Jasper now.

We were going to have to abort our mission. I just hoped that I'd be able to connect with the host later when I delivered the promised donuts.

It was the best I could do at the moment, anyway.

Or so I thought.

As I drove us away from the house, I noticed a lone man sitting on a concrete bench just off the drive. If I hadn't been looking in his direction, I might have easily missed him, but the moment I saw him, I knew that we'd had a stroke of luck at last.

It was Jasper Finney, and by the look of him, he wasn't having a very happy birthday at all.

"Jasper? What's wrong?" I asked as Grace and I approached him. He hadn't seen us stop the Jeep or park it on the grass either, and if he'd spotted us nearing him on foot, he didn't show it.

Jasper Finney looked up and stared at us both blankly for a moment, as though he were lost, even though he was still on his own property. The panic was gone in a moment, but it stuck in my mind.

"Hello, ladies. What brings you out here?" he asked as he tried to recover his wits about him.

"What's going on with you?" I repeated.

"Nothing," he said.

"Jasper," I insisted.

He shrugged a moment before explaining, "I suppose when you get to be my age, you begin to struggle with the question of your own mortality."

"Nonsense. Any man who insists on donuts as his birthday treat is going to live forever," I said, doing my best to cheer the man up. I'd never seen him so downcast in all the years that I'd known him, and I was getting more than a little worried about him.

"Frankly, if I live to see another sunrise, I'll be surprised," he said so softly that I almost didn't hear it.

"Are you in some kind of danger?" Grace asked him gently.

"Aren't we all, on one level or another?" he asked glumly. It wasn't exactly a straight answer, but I had a hunch that it was the best one we were going to get.

"Then why the dour prediction?" I asked him. "Frankly, it's not like you."

Jasper stared at his hands for a moment, and then when he looked back up at us, he did his best to fabricate a smile. "Of course it's not. You're right. It's just a case of the birthday blues." He narrowed his gaze at me for a moment before he added,

"You're not going to try to talk me out of giving you that bonus, are you?"

"I was going to," I admitted, "but Grace talked me out of it."

"Good for you," he told her, a true smile appearing for the first time since we'd stopped to chat with him. "You get it, don't you?"

"It's your birthday," Grace said with a grin. "As far as I'm concerned, you should have whatever you want, including overpaying Suzanne for her donuts." She paused a moment before adding, "I should correct that. Whatever you want within reason, of course."

"Ah, reason. There's the rub, isn't it? If I had any sense at all, I'd shut this farce down right now and send everyone on their way."

"Then that's exactly what you should do," I said as I reached into my pocket and pulled out the check I'd just gotten from Bethesda Long. "I haven't even started the donuts yet, so consider this visit on the house."

He refused the check, though. "As much as I appreciate your willingness to forego what must be a rather substantial paycheck for you, I'm afraid that wheels have been set into motion that cannot be stopped."

"If you ask me, there's *nothing* that we can't fix if we put our minds to it."

"I remember being that young once upon a time," he said wistfully with a slight smile. "Nothing seemed impossible back then. I honestly believed that I could slay any dragon that came my way."

"You still can," I said.

"I'm afraid those days are long gone." Jasper suddenly stood and slapped his hands together in a single loud clap. "Enough ramblings from an old fool," he said. "You need to get started on those donuts. It's the main thing I'm looking forward to tonight, so don't disappoint me, Suzanne."

"I'll try my best not to," I said. "Could we give you a ride back to the house?"

"No, but thank you for the kind offer. I aim to ramble, to stroll, and to lollygag my way back. If it takes me two hours, then so be it."

"You make it sound like so much fun I wish I could join you," I told him.

That got a real grin from him, and as he walked away from us toward the house at a snail's pace, he threw a hand over his shoulder, bidding us good bye.

"What do you make of that?" I asked Grace once we were back in the Jeep and heading toward Donut Hearts.

"The man seems genuinely depressed about something," she said.

"So you agree with me. It's more than the fact that he's just getting old," I answered as I swerved to miss a suicidal squirrel. That gave me a moment's pause. "You don't think he's going to kill himself tonight, do you?"

"What? Where did that come from?" Grace asked me as she glanced in my direction with a puzzled expression.

"I don't know. Maybe because of that squirrel that just darted in front of the Jeep or the way Jasper sounded just now. At his age, I can see where birthdays could be depressing."

"I'm not disagreeing with you, but if he was going to kill himself, why hold a party in the first place? I don't get it. Jasper doesn't seem the type of person who would enjoy long and morbid good-byes."

"You're probably right, but I just can't help thinking that *something* is going on with him," I said as we got back into town.

"Tell you what. Why don't we speak with him again at the party and see if he's lightened up any by then?"

"And if he hasn't?" I asked her as I pulled back into her driveway.

"Then we do our best to convince him that it's a very bad idea to be so glum during his remaining time on earth," Grace replied. "Come on. If being around the two of us doesn't make him want to see another day, I don't know what would."

Her infectious attitude was catching. "Okay, it's a deal. What are you going to do with the rest of your afternoon?"

"What I always do when I find myself with a minute of free time during working hours these days," she said glumly. "Paperwork."

"Is it really that bad?" I had my share of forms I had to deal with running Donut Hearts, from supply orders to permit reapplications to a dozen different other time wasters, but I couldn't imagine it taking up so much of my time. There were some real advantages to having a real job working for wages and getting insurance, but there were some perks for working on your own, too.

"It would make any sane person run screaming into the woods," Grace said, and then she patted my knee before she got out. "Don't worry about me, though. I'll find some way to deal with it. Besides, this year I qualify for another full week of paid vacation."

I looked at her as though I were confused. "I'm sorry, what did you just say? I get a day off every now and then, but are you telling me that someone actually pays you *not* to show up for work?"

"I know. It's crazy, isn't it?" she asked with a grin as she left the Jeep and walked inside, but not before stopping and waving at me like a maniac.

Grace was good for me. Her spirit had a way of buoying mine on the darkest occasions, and that was just one of the reasons she was my best friend. I knew that with her at the sleepover tonight, and Jake as well as Momma and Phillip, we were in for an interesting time.

I just hoped that Jasper Finney had a chance to enjoy himself as much as we all planned to.

But I was going to have to worry about that later.

For now, Emma and I had to make the donuts for the second time that day, and substantial bonus or not, it was rarely as much fun the second time around within such a short period of time.

CHAPTER 5

"YOU'RE ALREADY HERE," I SAID with surprise when I found Emma getting to work in the kitchen without me. She had already started getting out some of the supplies we'd be needing for the eighteen dozen donuts we'd be making, and my assistant looked a little guilty when she saw me.

"Sorry. I didn't think you'd mind," Emma apologized.

"You know what? I don't mind at all. Would *you* like to make the donuts this afternoon? I can be your assistant for a change."

"I wasn't trying to push you out," Emma said with a frown.

"Believe me, you aren't," I answered. "Come on. It might shake things up a little. Just don't get used to it, though," I said with a grin. "I don't want a power struggle on my hands. After all, when you're here with your mother, you're the boss."

"But you're not my mother," she said defensively.

"I know, but if you can manage to boss her around, I should be a breeze for you. I can't imagine telling *my* mother what to do."

Emma smiled at me. "I didn't have many problems with it, but it took her a few days to get used to the idea."

"Okay, then. We should be good," I said as I started helping her set up for the donut production schedule. "What do you want me to do first?"

"Well, if you're serious about letting me run the show this

afternoon, why don't you start folding boxes out front while I prep the yeast donut batter?"

"You actually start the raised donuts *before* you make the cake ones?" I asked her. It was completely opposite from my system, and I couldn't help myself. I'd had to ask.

"That's the way I normally do it, but if you have a problem with it, that's fine with me," she said. "If you want to take over, be my guest."

From the expression on her face, it would clearly *not* be okay for me to change my mind. "Sorry. I spoke out of turn. You're in charge. I'll go get started on those eighteen boxes. If you need me, just holler."

"Thanks. I'll let you know when it's time to start washing the first batch of dishes."

"You're going to really enjoy this, aren't you?" I asked her with a smile.

"If I told you it was almost worth giving up my cut of the profits, I'd be afraid you might take me up on it."

That reminded me. I'd forgotten that I hadn't brought her up to speed about our new, elevated payout for the afternoon's work. At the last second, I decided to keep that to myself, at least for the moment. Why not give her a surprise as well?

After the boxes were ready to accept their treats, I poked my head back into the kitchen. Emma had just finished dropping the last of the cake donuts, and she was already moving on to stage two in her yeast donut prep work. "Is it safe for me to come in?"

"I was just about to sound the all clear," she said.

I looked at her work so far and considered her system of making the donuts. "You know, I might just switch over to your method myself. The way I figure it, it would buy me another hour's worth of sleep every morning."

Emma grinned sheepishly at me. "That's why I came up with the idea in the first place," Emma admitted. "You don't mind, do you?"

"No, of course not." I looked over at the large stack of dirty pots and implements. "I'd better get started on those."

"I can pitch in if you'd like," she offered, but I just shook my head.

"No thanks. We're dividing the labor this afternoon, remember?" I honestly didn't mind washing up. It reminded me of the days when I worked alone at the shop. On one day out of every week, I still did everything, from making the first cake donut to washing the last dirty coffee mug, and everything in between. It always gave me a sense of satisfaction when I locked the door, but there was never a time I wasn't happy to have Emma back again the next day. As I lost myself in the sea of suds, I thought about the conversation Grace and I had shared with Jasper earlier. The man was normally a font of joy, spreading happiness wherever he went.

So what had changed?

I was still pondering the possibilities when Emma repeated my name.

I looked up from the nearly empty sink and grinned at her. "I must have zoned out there for a second."

"You don't have to tell me about the Zen of dishwashing," she said.

"What was it you wanted?" I asked her as I finished rinsing the last spatula.

"We have time for a ten-minute break, if you're interested," Emma offered.

"You bet I am." I drained the sink first, though, and rinsed out the sides before I was ready to go, something Emma never did when she washed dishes. We each had our own techniques, which was fine by me.

After she set the timer, I followed Emma out into the kitchen. "Do you mind if we sit inside today?" she asked me. "I know we usually like to take our breaks outside, but that's in the middle of the night. I don't feel like telling people that we're closed and disappointing them."

"I couldn't agree more," I said. "So, how was your time off this afternoon?"

I'd meant it as a joke, since we'd only had a few hours away from the place, but Emma missed my sarcasm completely. "Barton is going to set up a pop-up restaurant in a few weeks, and I've been helping him plan things so he'll be ready."

"I thought he was still working in the hospital cafeteria," I said. Emma's boyfriend, Barton Gleason, was a fine, well-trained chef who had taken a job cooking at the hospital when he couldn't find anything else. Since then, he'd been shocking and delighting the folks who came there to eat, but no one was foolish enough to believe that he was going to be there for the long term. In fact, he'd been nearly ready to accept a job offer in Charlotte working at a fancy restaurant when he and Emma had started dating. Since then, his talk about relocating had suddenly gone silent.

"He is, but if he can open his own place, that's what he really wants to do," Emma explained. "It's really quite fascinating how these pop-up events are announced on social media." Her voice trailed off the moment she realized that she'd lost my attention. "Sorry, I didn't mean to bore you," she said.

"You didn't. I'm the one who should be apologizing. I've just been thinking all afternoon about the party we're making these donuts for," I admitted. "Jasper is depressed, and I think it's more than just because he's getting another year older."

"I suppose I get it, but the party is really cranking up

everyone's interest. Dad's been collecting information about it since he first heard what Jasper was going to do. He's got dossiers on the family as well as Jasper's business associates ready for a special edition. It's killing him that he didn't score an invitation to the party itself, let alone the sleepover."

That was interesting. Ray Blake and I generally kept our distance, but if he had information I could use, maybe there was a way I could share a little of my own with him without compromising my principles too much. "Do you think your dad would be open to a little quid pro quo?" I asked her.

"Seriously? Suzanne, not to put too fine a point on it, but you've been trying to keep away from Dad for as long as I can remember."

She was right about that. "Okay. Forget it. He probably wouldn't have gone for it, anyway."

"Are you kidding? He'd leap at the chance. I just don't want you doing anything you might regret later." With a hint of a frown, she added, "And I certainly wouldn't want you to take it out on me if things went badly between you. You are both important parts of my life, and frankly, I don't like it when either one of you is mad at me."

I had a sudden thought. "Tell you what. Invite him over here right now. You can stay in the kitchen, and your father and I will chat out here. That way you're not involved in any way, shape, or form. How does that sound to you?"

"I'm willing to make the call, but are you sure that you want to do this?" she asked as she pulled her phone out.

"No, but since when has that stopped me in the past?" I asked her with a grin. She didn't match it, though. "I'm kidding, Emma. Call him."

She seemed reluctant to do it, but she made the call anyway.

Five minutes later, my assistant was back in the kitchen working alone, while I was sitting out front with her father, ready to make a deal with my very own devil if it would help me aid my friend.

"I was surprised to get Emma's call," the newspaperman said a little smugly as he sat across from me.

I decided to let it go, at least for the moment. "The truth is, I'm concerned about Jasper Finney, and I thought you might be able to help me get a handle on what's going on with him."

That softened Ray's posing. "I get that. Jasper has lived a long time, and it's been my experience when you do that, you seem to collect more than your share of enemies over the years."

"Seriously? I don't think that's true at all. My mother is no spring chicken, and I can't think of a single enemy she has," I said.

Ray looked at me steadily for a few moments before speaking again. "Suzanne, if something bad should ever happen to your mother, which I hope it never does, I'm afraid there would be quite a list of suspects. Don't forget, she's a powerful woman in this town, and she's not afraid to use it to get her way."

I wasn't about to sit there and listen to that nonsense. I stood up and moved to the front door. "This was a mistake. Sorry I wasted your time, but you need to go, Ray."

He looked baffled by my reaction, which was a surprise in and of itself to me. Did the man not realize how many negative things he'd just implied about my mother? I knew that Momma wasn't a saint by any means, but she wasn't some dastardly land baron leaving broken bodies and souls in her path, either.

"Suzanne, I didn't mean anything by it. I was just trying to prove my point."

"Oh, you proved it all right," I said, not wavering.

Emma poked her head out of the kitchen. "How's it going?" It took her less than a second that she hadn't needed to even ask the question. "Never mind, don't answer that. Dad, you need to apologize."

"Were you eavesdropping on our private conversation, Emma?" Ray asked his daughter pointedly.

"I didn't have to. I could tell the second I came out here that you said something to Suzanne that you shouldn't have. Dad, you really need to learn how to be better with people if you want them to cooperate with you."

"When I'm after a story, I do what needs to be done, no matter how unpleasant some folks might find it," Ray said, trying to defend his behavior.

"That's the thing though, Ray," I said. "I was going to offer you something valuable in return for a little information, but you tried to use it to patronize me and impugn my mother's character. I'm curious about something. How did you *think* I'd take you attacking Momma?"

"That's the problem. He didn't think about it at all," Emma said as she strode quickly over to the table. "Come on, Dad. You heard Suzanne. You're leaving."

"I was just trying to make a point," Ray protested. "Why is everyone getting so worked up about it?"

"Do I need to call Mom?" Emma threatened.

The mere threat was all that Ray needed. He practically jumped up from the booth and headed for the door, but before he would leave, he hesitated in front of me. "Suzanne, I'm honestly sorry about what I said earlier. I made a mistake. I should never have brought your mother into the conversation. Forgive me?"

When Ray said it like that, it was hard to stay angry at him, especially with Emma looking on. "I suppose I can let it slide this time."

"Good," he said, clearly grateful for the reprieve. "See? There's no need to bring your mother into this at all, Emma," Ray told his daughter.

"I guess not," she answered. "But you still need to go."

"Why? After all, we just patched things up," he said. "Suzanne still needs the information I have."

"It's up to you, but if it were me, I'd go ahead and throw him out," Emma said.

"Emma!" Ray protested.

"Hey, I'm just doing what I need to do, no matter how unpleasant some folks might find it," she said with a shrug.

"Point taken," he said, and finally, Ray started to leave.

I wasn't quite ready for him to go yet, though. "If I let you stay, will you do your best not to anger me again?" I asked him.

"I'll be a perfect angel," he said.

"Hah," Emma replied, clearly showing that she didn't believe him.

"Seriously?" Ray asked his daughter, who just shrugged in response.

"Thanks, Emma. How's it going in the kitchen?" I asked as I gestured toward the kitchen.

"I'm hopping, but I can handle it. How much more time do you need? Those dishes are really stacking up," she said with a grin.

It was clear Ray was puzzled by the comment, but he was also afraid to say anything.

"I'll be in soon. Just give me two minutes."

"Okay," my assistant said. As Emma walked back into the kitchen, she pointed to her eyes, and then she gestured toward her father. The intent was clear enough. Emma would be watching him, so he'd better be careful.

"What have you got on Jasper's family and friends?" I asked as Ray and I sat at the same table again. "You heard your daughter, so I'd appreciate it if you'd make it quick. Why would Jasper feel so blue on his birthday? Do they have anything to do with it?"

"They have everything to do with it, if you ask me," Ray

said. "Ethan's business is going under, and Bobby has a gambling problem. Phyllis has been engaged in some questionable activities, and Perry Kilroy has threatened to kill him on more than one occasion, and he's Jasper's best friend in the world. I'd say he had reason enough to feel sadness, given all of that."

"Is all of that true?" I asked Ray. "Or are they just theories of yours?"

"Sadly, it's all real enough. Ethan has walked away from his real estate business, and there are rumors that he misappropriated some of his sales staff's commissions along the way. I'm guessing that's why he's been doting on his grandfather. He's hoping the old man is going to bail him out. The same goes for his son, Bobby. The apple doesn't fall far from the tree, evidently. Bobby is in need of a serious cash infusion, or he's going to be in some serious trouble. I haven't been able to get a handle on Phyllis so far, but if half the things I've read about her are true, she's spending money at a much faster rate than she's taking it in. She's never had a real job, but her father left her quite a tidy sum. Unfortunately, that ran out some time ago. As for Kilroy, he's sued Jasper three times for various things, and he's lost every time. If he's his best friend, then Jasper's in some real need of new companionship."

"Thanks, Ray," I said as I started to stand. "You've been a big help."

"Hang on," Ray said. "Emma mentioned something about you returning the favor."

I was hoping he'd forgotten that, but clearly I was delusional. "Tell you what. I heard you wanted to go to the party."

"Can you get me in?" Ray asked hopefully.

"Not a chance. However, I can report back to you what happened, with a few conditions. You don't use my name, or any reference to me whatsoever, and you don't attack Jasper. He's got enough problems without you going after him. Understood?"

"I don't know. You're really tying my hands here," Ray complained.

"Sorry, but it's the best that I'm willing to do," I said, though it was clear to both of us that it wasn't at all true that I was remorseful about my offer. "Take it or leave it."

"Will you at least snap a few photos for me?" Ray asked as he pulled a small, spy-like camera out of his pocket. "No one will know what you're doing. Just get me some good shots, and we'll call it even."

I was tempted to take the camera just to play with it, but I didn't want to cross that line. "No photos."

"Then the deal's off," Ray said as he stood up. "I'd appreciate it if you'd let me out."

It was my turn to be surprised. "Are you serious? Just because I won't take some innocuous photos for you, you're going to slam Jasper anyway?"

"Hey, if that happens, just remember, his blood is on your hands," Ray said.

I had to make a decision, and I had to do it quickly. Shooting out my hand, I said, "Fine. Give me the camera."

Ray happily handed it over. "Don't forget, get some good shots. And I still want the scoop about what happened, too."

"I said yes," I said as I unlocked the door and let him out. I felt a little greasy taking covert photos for the newsman, but I was going to make sure that I "accidently" took harmless ones. If I had my say, he wouldn't be able to use any of them in his story. As to the recap I'd promised him, I'd make sure to tell him only what was freely available from common knowledge and to be sure to provide nothing that would hurt my friend.

Based on what Ray had just told me, Jasper Finney had enough problems without me piling on, too.

CHAPTER 6

"I'M SORRY ABOUT MY FATHER," Emma said as I walked back into the kitchen alone.

"You have nothing to apologize for," I told her as I started in on the next batch of dishes. Emma seemed to produce a great deal of dirty pots and pans when she made donuts, but I wasn't about to complain about it. It was honestly kind of nice having a break from making donuts and yet still being there where I belonged.

"I know he can get a little intense sometimes," she said. "Was he very helpful to you?"

"He gave me some information that I wasn't aware of before," I admitted.

"But..." Emma said.

"But what?"

"What did you have to give up in return? My dad is a firm believer in the maxim that there's no such thing as a free lunch."

"I promised to tell him about the party," I said, hedging my involvement in case something came up later.

Emma looked at me sternly. "I thought we were going to be honest with each other. I know my father. That wouldn't have been enough to get him to agree to help you."

"He wants me to take some photos, as well," I admitted.

"You at least asked to be anonymous, didn't you?" she asked me.

"Of course I did."

"Even in the photo credits?" she followed up.

"That never even occurred to me," I said. "Would he really do that?"

She nodded glumly. "He would, and he will. Don't give him those pictures until you have his word that your name won't appear anywhere in his newspaper for a full week."

"Will he make that kind of blanket promise?" I asked her, amazed by how well my assistant knew her dad.

"If you start off with a month, he'll offer you three days. A week should be an easy compromise to get. Would you like me to broker the agreement for you?"

"No, I think I can handle it," I said as I turned off the warm water and added the soap.

"Okay, but if you get in trouble, don't hesitate to call me."

"I won't," I said as I examined a small bowl with something red still in it. "Raspberry filling?"

"No, it's cherry. I tried to make some of our favorites, and then I threw in a few just for Jasper. He loves cherry filled, doesn't he?"

"On occasion, but cranberry are his favorite," I admitted. I looked at the cake donut offerings and saw that Emma had already made sour cream, old-fashioned, chocolate, and indeed, cranberry as well. For the yeast donuts, she'd already prepared the cherry filling and was just getting started on the lemon. "Would you like me to pitch in and lend you a hand?"

"Thanks, but I've got it covered," she said.

I looked around at the progress in real amazement. "You really do. Wow, sometimes I forget just how good you've become at making donuts. You aren't bored when you work as my assistant, are you?"

"No. Quite honestly, I'm happy for the break. Running this place twice a week is plenty enough for me. When I'm back at my regular job at the sink, I enjoy the opportunity to take life at a slower pace. I don't know how you manage on your own on my day off."

"Are you volunteering to work seven days a week?" I asked her with a smile.

"Not a chance, but I'll be careful before I take another full day off in the future."

"Emma, I really don't mind if you use your vacation. There's a certain rhythm I get in when I'm working by myself."

"Still, it's got to be exhausting," she said as she finished dropping the last of the yeast donuts. As soon as they were out, she glazed them and set them aside to finish her two fillings. By the time she'd be done, they'd be ready to fill. I'd made the mistake once of filling yeast donuts while they were still hot, and I'd had an incredibly gooey mess on my hands afterwards.

In no time at all, all eighteen dozen donuts were finished. "Whew, that was a lot of work, but at least we're being paid handsomely for it," Emma said with a sigh.

"Better than you realize," I said as I pulled out the check and handed it to Emma.

She whistled softly when she saw the amount. "That's quite a bit more than we were expecting," she said.

"What can I say? Jasper felt generous, it being his birthday and all. Why don't you drop it off at the bank on your way home? I'll cut you a check right now for your half, after expenses, if you'd like."

"That's okay. It can wait," she said.

"Why don't you let me do it now? You want to go shopping, and some extra cash could be nice to have. Give me two minutes, and I'll figure out our expenses and your half."

"I'll start cleaning up a little while you're doing that," she volunteered.

"You don't have to. That wasn't part of our deal."

"With what I'm making, it's the least I can do," she said with a hearty grin. "You're a great boss, Suzanne."

"Why? Because I'm cutting you in on the profits for working overtime?"

"That's certainly one reason," she said with a nod, "but there are a bunch more than that. The fact is that I love working here."

"Well, as long as I own Donut Hearts, you've got a place by my side."

I began doing the math, and I soon had a substantial figure for Emma's portion of the proceeds. It was fun writing her the check, made even better by the fact that I was getting an equal amount. I never would have dreamed of keeping the lion's share of the proceeds for our additional work, though it may have made the best financial sense. Splitting the largesse with her was what was right, at least in my mind, and that made it the only option I saw myself having.

After Emma was off to the bank, I finished up the last few chores and then headed home. I decided to leave the donuts on the counter and retrieve them later. Jake and I would have to pass by the shop on our way to the party, but before I was ready to head out to Jasper's place, I needed a shower, a change of clothes, and time to pack an overnight bag.

Thirty minutes later, I felt like a brand new gal. I was clean, I didn't reek of donuts, and I had my husband beside me. The donuts were loaded into bins now in the back of Jake's truck, and we were on our way.

"We don't have much time, so there's something I need to tell you before we get there," I said as he drove.

"The way I figure it, you've got about seven minutes, so you'd better make it quick," Jake said.

"I made a deal with Ray Blake this afternoon," I said, and I could already see my husband begin to cloud up. Jake was not a big fan of the newspaperman. In fact, the only reason my husband tolerated him at all was because of the way he felt about Emma and her mother, Sharon. "Before you lose your temper, know that I didn't feel as though I had any choice. Jasper's been acting really strange lately, and I'm worried about him, especially given this party he's throwing."

"Why is a party the sign of a *bad* thing?" Jake asked me.

"He's clearly not in the mood for it. It almost feels as though he's going to try to settle some old scores, and I wanted to be forewarned in case I was needed."

Jake nodded reluctantly. "Well, if you were after gossip, rumor, and innuendo, you went straight to the source. What did Ray have to say?"

Once I caught Jake up on my list of the folks with problems with Jasper, I finished by saying, "It doesn't sound like a very happy life to me. Does it to you?"

"No, not all that much. What did you have to give Ray in return?"

"A recap of the party, and some pictures taken with this," I said as Jake pulled down the lane to Jasper's house.

He glanced at the camera, and then he looked at it again. "That's meant to take surveillance photos," Jake said. "You're not actually going to do it, are you?"

"Actually, I was hoping that *you* would," I said as I put it on his lap. "Our goal is to provide Ray with photos, but nothing he could possibly print. Do you feel up to the task?"

"Why not? It could be fun," Jake said as he slipped the camera into his pocket. "Where do I park? I don't particularly want to lug all those bins of donuts very far."

"You won't have to. Follow the signs around back for support staff," I instructed him.

"That's sensible enough," Jake replied, and he did as I instructed.

"Bethesda seems to be very good at what she does," I said.

As we carried the first load of donuts into the kitchen area, Angelica and Sophia were both hard at work. They barely had time to say hello, and the matriarch talked as she worked. "We're taking off in a few minutes. Antonia called and said that they've got some kind of kitchen emergency I need to see to."

"Is there anything we can do to help?" I asked, volunteering our services without even consulting Jake. I knew that I didn't have to. He was as big a fan of the DeAngelis women and their restaurant as I was.

"No, we're nearly finished here," she said. As she took in my offerings, she added, "Those look amazing."

"Emma made them," I admitted with more than a little pride in my voice.

"Which is an even greater compliment to your skills, if you can teach someone so thoroughly to replace you," she replied. "It is ultimately my goal, but unfortunately, the end is nowhere in sight."

"I'm standing right here, you know," Sophia said. "It's not like I can't hear you."

"You were meant to hear every word of it," Angelica said with a wry grin.

"Whatever," Sophia said. "We need to step it up, Mom."

"I know that," she said as Bethesda Long came bustling in. The party planner spotted me, ignoring Jake completely. "Those go in the sitting room, two doors down." With that, she dismissed us both as she turned to Angelica. "Where do we stand?"

"Two minutes, and we'll be through," she said.

"I really wish at least one of you would stay behind," Bethesda said reprovingly.

"And I find myself wishing for another daughter to ease

my load, but unfortunately, neither of us are going to get our fondest desires."

"I'm telling the other girls what you just said," Sophia said as she tasted a pot of simmering sauce. As she reached for a canister filled with some kind of herb, Angelica stopped her.

"It needs a little more oregano," Sophia protested.

Angelica raised one eyebrow and then put a fresh spoon into the pot. After a moment, she nodded. "So, add it."

"You're really okay with me adjusting your recipe?" Sophia asked, clearly startled by the development.

"I'm not arrogant enough to think that I'm the only good cook in the family," she replied.

That was all we heard, as Bethesda shooed us out of the kitchen.

"Those two are a pair, aren't they?" Jake asked as we carried another load into the sitting room.

"They're too much alike, and neither one of them can see it in the other," I agreed.

Once the donuts were all transferred, we removed them from their bins and placed them on fine sterling silver trays.

My donuts, or rather, Emma's, had never had such an elegant presentation.

"What do we do now?" Jake asked me as we put the empty bins back into his truck bed. It had taken us ten minutes, but for now, or at least until it was time for the party to officially begin, we were on our own.

"Now we find Jasper and see how he's doing," I said, leading my husband back inside.

We'd barely made it through the door though when we heard people arguing, so naturally, that's straight where Jake and I headed.

CHAPTER 7

"YOU SHOULDN'T EVEN BE HERE, Perry," a blustering older woman said. It was Phyllis Carlisle, Jasper's granddaughter, and my mother's once-upon-a-time rival for my father's affections. In the intervening years since I'd last seen her, time had not been her friend. She must have gained forty pounds since I'd last seen her, but she was still trying to wear clothes that had been made for women much younger than she was. At her side was a mousy little fellow at least fifteen years her junior, and by the way he held onto her, I had to assume that he was her latest amour.

"Be that as it may, here I am," the man she'd been arguing with replied calmly. He looked to be every bit as old as Jasper was, and I would have had no clue as to who he was if Ray hadn't briefed me earlier. It had to be Perry Kilroy, Jasper's former partner. "In fact, Jasper invited me himself. He said there was something he wanted to discuss with me, and I decided to indulge him, given our long history."

"Your history includes you threatening to kill him!" Phyllis said loudly.

"Now, dear, remember your blood pressure," the man beside her said indulgently.

"Henry, please kindly butt out. This is none of your affair," she said, slapping him down quite thoroughly with her stinging words.

I half expected Henry to protest, but he simply stepped

away from Phyllis's dominant personality and kept any further protestations to himself.

"Perhaps you should follow your own advice," Perry said with an evil little grin. "After all, we'd hate to have you stroke out on such an important occasion."

"*I'm* not the one who's in danger," she said softly.

"Is that a threat, child?" Perry asked her. If I had to guess, I would say that he looked rather amused by her statement instead of being alarmed.

"I'm not your child!" she snapped.

"No, of course not. If you were, you'd be much better behaved."

Suddenly Phyllis lunged for him, and to my surprise, Jake didn't even have to step in. Mousy little Henry managed to restrain her all by himself, though I wasn't at all certain how long he could manage it.

Evidently Perry decided that discretion was the better part of valor, because he quickly excused himself. "I'm going to have a word with Jasper before this nonsense goes any further."

"We'll come with you," I said on impulse.

He turned to stare at me before replying. "And who might you be?"

"Don't pay any attention to her. She's not important. She's just a donut maker," Phyllis said as dismissively as she could manage.

I could feel my husband tense beside me, but the last thing I needed at the moment was to have him leap to defend my honor. "And don't forget, I'm a long-term friend of Jasper's as well. We were just off to find him. The more the merrier, don't you agree?"

Perry Kilroy had no choice but to allow it, since Jake and I were going with him, regardless of how he might feel about it. "Very well," he said reluctantly.

"We're going, too," Phyllis said. "After all, *I'm* the only *real* family he has left."

"What about Ethan and Bobby?" I asked innocently.

"They are a pair of bloodsucking leeches, like father, like son. They don't love my grandfather the way I do."

"I'm curious about something," I said as we all started upstairs. "I can't remember the last time you were in town to visit him."

"That's because I don't stop in at your donut shop every time I come to see my grandfather," she said haughtily.

Based on her figure, I doubted that was the case, but I decided not to pursue it. We made our way up to the master suite, but the door was wide open, and what was more, it was empty.

"He's not here," Henry said gently.

"Brilliant observation," Phyllis told her beau as she turned to leave the room.

"Where are you going?" Perry asked her.

"To his inner sanctuary, of course," Phyllis said. "If he's not here resting, then he must be in his study."

"I don't know if that's really true. I saw him taking a walk outside earlier this afternoon," I admitted.

Phyllis looked at me as though she wanted to choke me for daring to dispute her, but I just grinned at her in return. Jake must have found the exchange amusing, because I heard him stifle a chuckle beside me, one Phyllis clearly chose to ignore. After the others left, my husband lingered a bit, pulled out Ray's spy camera when no one was looking, and took a few shots of the bedroom, the hallway, and the chandelier.

Our little caravan made it downstairs and to what had to be Jasper's study, though I'd never been there myself. This door was closed, and locked as well, and I noticed my husband take a photo of it as Henry tried the knob and then knocked repeatedly. I watched in amusement as Jake also took a shot of the garish carpet runner in the hallway. Let Ray try to use that in his newspaper article.

"He's clearly not here, either," Henry said. I was amazed the man ever dared speak at all, given the amount of rebukes he must have received on a daily, if not hourly, basis.

Phyllis was frowning, though. "That's odd. He almost never locks this door," she said.

"Never? That's a rather broad blanket statement, isn't it?" Perry asked her.

"Not if you know my grandfather at all. You two were partners for a great many years, so you should have at least been aware of that particular habit of his," she answered, and then she reached under a nearby potted plant and plucked out a key. "There are only two keys to that lock. One is on his person at all times, and the other he keeps here for emergencies."

"And you believe that this actually qualifies as an emergency?" Perry asked her wryly.

"He's missing, isn't he? Besides, we won't know until we check it out, will we?" Phyllis asked as she brushed Henry aside and put the key in place in the lock.

Turning the knob, she threw the door open and started to say, "Jasper, are you..."

There was no reason for her to finish her sentence, though.

Jasper would clearly never be anything again but dead.

Evidently his feeling of doom had been well-founded after all.

CHAPTER 8

"IS HE DEAD?" PHYLLIS ASKED despite what we were all seeing. Someone had taken a letter opener, one that looked to be thick and heavy, and they'd driven it into Jasper Finney's chest, impaling him with it in his own leather chair.

Jake stepped forward and checked for a pulse anyway, though the dead stare on Jasper's face and the ashen complexion were enough to tell me that he was well beyond our help. My husband checked anyway as he instructed me, "Call 9-1-1."

I did as he suggested, and after I got the dispatcher on the line, I said, "There's been a murder at the Finney estate. Jake Bishop has confirmed that the victim is dead," I added as I looked at Jake, who nodded his head sadly as he stood up from the body.

Phyllis made a move toward her late grandfather, and as her hand reached out for the letter opener, Jake restrained her.

"Don't touch a thing," he said as the dispatcher said the same thing to me.

"We can't just leave him like that," Phyllis protested, struggling against my husband's firm grip.

"I'm truly sorry, but that's *exactly* what we're going to do," Jake said, and then he looked over at Henry, clearly looking for help that he wasn't going to get.

I hung up and decided to step in instead. "Come on. Let's get you out of here. You don't need to see this, Phyllis," I said as I coaxed her out of the room. Her companion was being absolutely worthless, his gaze stuck on the man's dead body. "How about a little help here, Henry? Henry!"

That got his attention. "Come, Phyllis. Let's get you some water."

"What I need is alcohol," she said numbly.

"I'm sure we can handle that as well," he answered.

Once they were both out of the room, it was just Perry, Jake, and me. Jasper's former partner stared at him for a second before joining the others. I couldn't tell what the expression on his face meant. It was almost as though he'd somehow been expecting this ultimate end for his former partner, however unlikely that might have been.

Then it was just the two of us.

"What do you make of it?" I asked Jake softly, as though speaking up might disturb Jasper in some way.

My husband examined the wound, being careful not to touch anything, and after a moment, he studied Jasper's body, as well as taking in its surroundings. Jake was currently in full-on "inspector" mode, and it was fascinating to watch him evaluate the crime scene. After a few moments, he said, "There may be fingerprints on the handle, but I'm not putting too much hope there. From the look of things, Jasper was struck from behind, so it was someone he trusted enough to turn his back on."

"How can you possibly know that?" I asked him.

"Look at the angle of the letter opener," he said. "It's pointing slightly downward and to the right side." Jake made a motion of stabbing the air, and I could see what he was saying, much too clearly for my taste. "If it had been from the front, the angle and the cant would both be different."

"Do you think Chief Grant will see that?" I asked. The chief was young, but that didn't mean that he wasn't good at his job.

The only reason I said it was because Jake had a great deal of experience on the state level.

"I'll make sure that he does. We'll have a little chat when he gets here," Jake said as he looked around. "I don't see anything else that looks out of place."

I pulled out my cell phone and started taking pictures of Jasper, the blade, and our surroundings. I took them from every angle, including from behind the murder victim looking out into the hallway, as well as out the window and toward the bookcase, a monstrosity made of quarter-sawn oak that must have weighed a ton. I caught glimpses of the trees outside the window, as well as the lawn, parts of the garish gold-and-green carpet runner in the hallway, and at least a dozen different hardcover thriller novels in the bookcase. It appeared that Jasper had enjoyed his fiction rough and tumble, whereas I liked mine gentle and cozy. I often said that when it came to my reading preferences, the small town and its locals I enjoyed reading about were very nearly ideal, if it weren't for all of the dead bodies, at any rate.

"Are we going to investigate this murder ourselves?" Jake asked when he saw what I was doing.

"How can we not? I *knew* Jasper was in trouble, and yet I did nothing about it. I feel somewhat responsible for what happened to him."

Jake took my hand in his after I put my cell phone away. "Unless you plunged that blade into his heart, you can't hold yourself responsible for what happened here," he said.

"I know that, but he was clearly crying out for help."

"And you were doing your best to provide it," Jake said. "There's no way you could have predicted this was going to happen." He glanced around, and then he asked me, "Should I take some shots of the crime scene for Ray? He's going to be screaming for some, you know."

"Take some that are out of focus, or pointing at the wrong

things," I suggested. "If he asks me, I'll tell him that I was so shaken up by what I saw that my hands were unsteady."

"Good idea," Jake said as he did as I suggested.

A moment later, there was a ruckus at the study door, and I looked up to see Ethan and Bobby Finney rushing into the room.

"What do you think you're doing?" Ethan asked in protest.

"We're securing the crime scene," Jake said as he shoved the camera back into his pocket.

"Grandpa," Ethan said, his voice fading as he took in the scene. "Is he dead?" he asked as he studied Jasper's lifeless body.

"Come on, Dad. There's nothing we can do for him," Bobby said as he pulled at his father's arm.

Was it my imagination, or was the younger Finney unable to look directly at the body of the family patriarch? Was that significant in any way?

"Somebody needs to call the police," Ethan said as we all heard sirens approaching.

"That would be them," Jake said. "We've got this under control."

Ethan made a move toward the old man's body, but Jake was clearly not having that, so he backed off quickly.

Chief Grant came in thirty seconds later and said automatically, "Please clear the room."

Ethan and Bobby started to go, but Jake and I stood our ground.

Ethan noticed our reluctance to leave immediately. "If they can stay, then so can we."

The chief shrugged. "He's right. Suzanne, would you mind stepping outside?"

"What about him?" Bobby asked as he pointed an accusatory finger at Jake.

"He's the former police chief and a retired state investigator. That makes him more than capable of assisting me at the crime scene." The way Chief Grant said it, there was no room for debate.

"Let's all wait outside," I said as I put a hand on each man's shoulder and herded them outside. Once we were in the hallway, the study door was firmly closed, and we were on the outside, wondering what was going on just on the other side of it.

Ethan started to break down after a moment. "I spoke with him less than an hour ago in the kitchen," he said, fighting back his sobs. "He was perfectly fine then."

"It's not like he was coming down with something," I said. I realized how callous it must have sounded the moment I said it. "I'm sorry for your loss. Both of you."

"Thanks," they said in unison.

"When was the last time that *you* saw him, Bobby?" I asked.

"It must have been at lunch," he said. "Why do you want to know that?"

"Just curious," I said. I had established a time of death, or at least a window of less than an hour. That might help in the investigation. Then again, it was a big house, a great many folks were there, and there was no way to say who had a solid alibi and who didn't.

"You don't think for one second that my son did this, do you?" Ethan asked, enraged by the mere suggestion that Bobby had played any part in what had happened to Jasper.

"Why? Did he have a motive?" I knew about the gambling debts, but I wasn't sure I was ready for them to know I knew quite yet.

"Of course not, and neither did I," he said angrily. "Why would we kill him?"

"If I had to guess, I'd say that a presumed inheritance might be reason enough," I replied, searching for some kind of reaction from either one of them.

I got one, but it was slightly delayed, as though Ethan had

weighed the level of response before he acted. When he did, he took three quick steps toward me, doing his best to cow me into submission.

If that was indeed his aim, he was out of luck. I'd faced down killers before, and I wasn't about to let him intimidate me. If anything, it only served to make me more determined to find out the truth. "Take that back. We didn't need his money."

I couldn't let that smug expression on his face stand, even though it may have been in my best interests to keep my knowledge to myself. "So then, are you saying that it's *not* true that your real estate firm is going bankrupt and that you've been appropriating funds that don't belong to you? Does that also mean that Bobby doesn't have a stack of gambling debts that are reaching untenable heights?"

I couldn't have scored two more direct hits if I'd slapped each man simultaneously. "Where did you hear that?" Ethan asked me in a whisper.

"A little birdie told me," I replied. "I'm curious about Jasper's will, though. Have either one of you happened to have seen a copy of it?"

They both looked at me with such anger that I was beginning to wonder about the wisdom of going after them so directly. To my relief, the study door opened just then and Jake stepped out, being careful to close it behind him.

"What's going on out here?" he asked, sizing up the situation instantly.

"You'd better muzzle your woman," Ethan said threateningly.

Jake didn't like that one bit. He got up in Ethan's face, mere inches from him, and said, "First of all, Suzanne is her own woman, and no one else's. Second, I pity the man who ever tried to muzzle her. My guess is that they'd pull back stubs instead of fingers, but if you think you're up to the task, you're more than welcome to try. The only thing is, though, that you'll have to get past me first. So, what do you say? Are you interested in having a go of it?"

Ethan clearly didn't want to tangle with Jake. "Come on, Bobby. I need some fresh air."

His son trailed along behind him without a word.

"What did you say to them, Suzanne?" Jake asked me.

"I'm sorry. I couldn't take their innocent acts, so I mentioned that Ethan was going bankrupt and Bobby had a great deal of gambling debts. You should have seen their faces when they realized I knew what I was talking about. Ray's information really paid off."

"In more ways than you know. I already shared it with the chief, too," he said calmly.

"I know I shouldn't have pushed them, but I did find out the last time either man admitted to seeing Jasper alive," I said.

"Go on." It was clear that Jake was a little unhappy with how I'd handled things, but he'd have to get over it. I'd done what I'd felt had been needed at the time, and there was no going back now, even if I wanted to.

"Bobby claims that he last saw Jasper at lunch, while Ethan says that he saw him an hour before we found the body. What did the chief say about your theory of Jasper being stabbed from behind?"

"He's taking it under consideration," Jake said with a shrug.

"Doesn't he realize that you are better at this than he is?" I asked. I'd long been a fan of Stephen Grant, and no one had cheered louder when he'd finally been made permanent police chief, but that didn't mean I thought he was in any way better or more qualified for his job than my husband was.

"Take it easy. He's a good cop," Jake said, defending him.

"Should we tell him what I just discovered?" I asked.

"Let me do it," Jake said. "I know you're the one who found out, but if you're in the room with me, I'm going to have to tell him that the father-and-son team know that we have information about motives for them both."

"You're not going to keep it from him, are you?" I asked.

"No, but I'd like to tell it to him in my own way, without interruption or justification," he admitted. "Do you have a problem with any of that?"

"No, that's fine by me," I replied. Jake was right. I'd get emotional if I was in the room. Let him handle this one.

"Good. Hang around, though. I'll be right back." Jake knocked on the study door, and then after a moment, he walked back inside.

I was left in the hallway, where Bethesda Long found me ten seconds later.

"I need to see Jasper," she said brusquely. "Is he in there?"

"Yes, but you can't speak with him," I said. Evidently the party planner hadn't heard the news of her boss's demise yet.

"Nonsense. I wouldn't ask if it weren't important. Now step aside."

She was about to knock on the door when I said, "Bethesda, somebody killed him. I'm afraid that Jasper Finney is dead."

"No. It can't be," she said as she started to fall onto the ornately patterned carpet runner in the hallway. Only the nearby wall kept her erect. Somehow she managed to right herself after brushing the floor with both hands. "Murder? Who would do such a thing? I spoke with him half an hour ago, and he was fine," she mumbled. "In fact, Angelica and I told him that the DeAngelis women were leaving. He seemed content, almost resigned to the fact that the party was going forward."

"Was there ever any doubt?" I asked her.

She frowned before she spoke again. "An hour ago, he approached me and said that it was a bad idea, that he wanted to end it before it began. I thought he was just getting cold feet, so I did my best to talk him out of cancelling, and ultimately, I succeeded. I was just coming to tell him that everything was set, and now you tell me that he's dead. I just can't bring myself to believe it."

"It's true enough," I said. "I saw the body."

"What happened? Was he shot? I never heard a firearm go off."

"What makes you think it was a gun?" I asked her, curious about her leap of reasoning.

"Isn't that how most people are murdered these days?" she asked. "If he wasn't shot, then how was he killed?"

There was no reason to try to keep that information to myself, since quite a few people already knew about it. "He was stabbed in the chest with a letter opener," I said.

"Oh, dear," she said. "I suppose this means that the party will be cancelled after all."

Was she seriously still concerned about the dead man's birthday party, even after what had just happened? I knew some people could be focused on their own jobs to the point where everything else was shaded out, but this was crazy. "There's not going to be a party. I'm sure the police will turn folks away as they try to come down the drive."

"What are we going to do with all of that food? And what about your donuts?"

"I could care less about any of that," I said. "Donate everything to the soup kitchen, for all I care. I know Jasper was quite fond of that particular cause, so it would have pleased him. My friend is dead. That's all I can think about right now."

"Of course," Bethesda said, getting her wits about her again. "I've known of Jasper for many years, but this was the first time I had the privilege to work for him." She lowered her voice as she added, "You should go straight to the bank and cash that check. I don't know what's going to happen with his estate, but you deserve to be paid for your services."

"Don't worry about that. It's already in the bank," I admitted.

"That was quick," she said.

"I had my assistant drop it into our account after we finished the work," I admitted. "Are you going to get paid for your services?"

She nodded. "It's already been taken care of as well. Now if you'll excuse me, I must go see about shutting things down."

"I wouldn't do anything until the police speak with you first, if I were you," I said.

"Why would they want to talk to *me*?" she asked, clearly confused about the possibility of being interviewed. "Do you know something that I don't?"

"At this point, I can't imagine it," I said. "I'm just guessing, but I have a feeling that every last one of us is going to be a suspect in Jasper Finney's murder."

"Even you?" she asked me incredulously.

"Even me," I acknowledged. "You, too."

"This is ridiculous," she said as four officers and two EMTs hurried into the hallway. I pointed them to the study, and they quickly disappeared inside. "I'll be in the kitchen if anyone needs me."

"That sounds like a solid plan to me," I said. At least Momma and Phillip hadn't arrived for the party yet, or Grace, either. They wouldn't be buried under clouds of suspicion like Jake and I were sure to be. I doubted that anyone would actually think that we'd kill Jasper, but then again, the rumor mill around town wasn't exactly based on intellect and sound reasoning.

I tried to think of something I could do while Jake was inside with the other professionals working the case.

Then it occurred to me that I had information about when each of my other suspects had seen the victim last, with the exception of Phyllis Carlisle and Perry Kilroy. I wasn't sure if Chief Grant would appreciate me gathering facts before he had a chance to, but I wasn't going to not investigate Jasper's murder. Thinking of his demise reminded me of the envelope he'd slipped into my hands just the day before, along with the warning not to open it unless he was dead. What did it say, this missive from beyond the grave? Was it a clue as to who might want him dead, or was it something a great deal more mundane? I didn't know, and I wouldn't until I made it back to the donut shop. I'd jammed the letter into my apron pocket, and as far as I knew, that's where it still was. I'd have to retrieve it sooner rather than later, though, now that Jasper was dead.

It might just help me find the man's killer.

CHAPTER 9

I GAVE JAKE THREE MORE MINUTES, but that was as long as I could stand to wait. My husband could always call me when he got himself free, and in the meantime, I could start doing a little more preliminary investigation on my own.

I found Phyllis first, sitting in the parlor with Henry by her side. Taking a seat across from them, I asked her, "Are you feeling any better?"

"I just lost my grandfather," she said as she stared at me dully. "How do you think I feel?"

"I'm sorry for your loss," I repeated, sharing the same sentiment with her that I had with her brother and nephew. "I lost my dad a long time ago, and I never really knew either of my grandfathers."

"This isn't about you, Suzanne," she said accusingly.

"Of course it's not. I just wanted to show you that I'm sympathetic to your situation. When was the last time you saw Jasper?"

"This morning," Phyllis said. "We had breakfast together."

"That's not quite true, dear," Henry said, much to the surprise of both of us.

"Are you calling me a liar?" she asked him, her words bristling with anger.

"Of course not," he said meekly. "But we did see him when we were out in the garden just after lunch. Remember?"

"Yes, but I hardly call that a meeting. We exchanged hellos, and then he went about his way. It was clear that something was on my grandfather's mind, and he was in no mood to talk to us, or anyone else, for that matter."

So, Phyllis had just lied to me about when she'd last seen the murder victim. Had it just slipped her mind, or was she trying to disguise the fact that she'd seen him so recently? "What was on his mind?" I asked.

"How should I know?" she snapped at me again. "I'm not a mind reader, and my grandfather could be quite cryptic when it suited him. He's been so sullen lately."

"Funny, but he was at the donut shop yesterday, and he didn't seem morose at all to me."

"That's because you were feeding his sugar cravings," Phyllis said. "Henry and I eat only healthy foods now, and we both feel so much better. Don't we, Henry?"

"Yes, dear," he said, though I doubted the sincerity of his own commitment.

"I understand you've had a few reversals lately," I said, trying to get information from her about her financial status.

"Merely ups and downs of the market," she said, trying to flick me off as though I were some kind of gnat that was starting to annoy her. If she thought I was being a pain so far, she had no idea what was in store for her in the future. "It happens to us all, occasionally."

"Funny, but I heard that every last dime of your previous inheritance was already gone," I said softly.

"Whoever told you that was lying, plain and simple," she said as she looked at me with a guarded gaze.

"Still, a cash infusion won't be unwelcome, if you're going to be getting one, that is."

It was a callous thing for me to say if she was innocent, but if she'd killed her grandfather for her share of her inheritance, it was a well-deserved barb.

Only time would tell which it was.

"Why wouldn't I receive a portion? After all, I'm family," she said.

"But you don't know for sure one way or the other. Is that right?"

"I refuse to sit here and have this conversation with a donut maker," Phyllis snapped, as though using my chosen profession to refer to me was some kind of insult. I couldn't have been more complimented by it than if she'd added that I was a pretty, pretty princess as well.

Phyllis stood and stormed off, but to my surprise, Henry didn't immediately join her. Instead, he sat right where he was and stared hard at me, showing a spine that I hadn't been at all sure that he'd even had. "You need to watch your step, Mrs. Hart."

"Actually, it's Ms.," I corrected him. "These questions are bound to be asked by the police. She must realize that she's a suspect, doesn't she?"

"What she does or does not know is none of your business, and you need to keep it that way," he said. Where had the formerly mousy companion gone? I wasn't sure, but Henry was showing me a completely different side of his personality. Was it possible that he might have killed Jasper himself to save Phyllis from financial ruin? I hadn't thought so before, but now I was beginning to have my doubts.

Evidently Phyllis finally noticed that her sycophant hadn't joined her. She marched back into the room and looked down at her companion with an expression of disdain. "Why are you still here?" she asked him archly, doing her best to ignore me.

"Coming, dearest," he said as he quickly joined her, but not before shooting me one last warning look.

"That was interesting," Perry Kilroy said from the other

room. I hadn't even realized that he'd been eavesdropping on our conversation until he spoke up.

"How much of that did you hear?" I asked him.

"Enough," he admitted. "I didn't think the milquetoast had it in him."

"To be honest with you, neither did I."

"You raised a valid point, though," Perry said. "I wouldn't doubt if Jasper's other progeny had equal financial motivations to get rid of him themselves."

"So then, you think he was murdered for his money?" I asked him.

"Why else? When you get to be our age, there's not much other reason to be killed for. It's not like he was cheating with another man's wife, is it?"

"I wouldn't rule it out because of his age," I said. "But I can't see Jasper doing something like that in any case. Can you?"

"It's honestly hard to say. The man had a habit of always surprising me when we were partners," Perry said. "Why should his death be any different?"

"There are other motives for murder besides greed, you know," I said with a frown.

"Is there something you'd like to say to me, young lady?" Kilroy asked pointedly.

"You two had so much bad blood between you that it's a wonder Jasper invited you here at all. What really puzzles me, though, is why you accepted the invitation."

"Does it really matter at this point?" Perry asked as he waved a hand in the air.

"It does to me, and I'm pretty sure that it will to the police, as well," I replied.

"Well, I'll tell you the same thing that I'll tell them if I'm asked. Jasper and I were in the process of forgiving past sins and putting all of that behind us. It's unfortunate that someone stole that opportunity from us, and personally, I'd like to see them punished for their actions."

"When was the last time you saw him?" I asked.

He merely smiled. "That, too, is none of your business, and I believe that I've indulged you quite enough for one day."

"I just have one more question," I said before he could get away.

He turned to face me before leaving. "And what might that be? If you're asking me if I killed him, the answer is no."

"Thanks, but that isn't what I'm curious about. I know a lot of partners take out insurance on each other's lives in case something happens to one of them."

"True, but don't forget, we haven't been in business together for a very long time," Perry said.

"Maybe so, but that doesn't mean that you let your insurance policy lapse. What will the police find when they start digging into that?" I asked.

Perry Kilroy didn't even bother responding. Instead, he turned and left through the French doors to go outside.

"What was that all about?" Jake asked me half a second later. Why were people constantly sneaking up on me? Were they trying to give me a heart attack?

"I just asked him a few innocent questions," I said, trying my best to look blameless in any way.

"I bet they were innocent," Jake said with a smile. "Are you ready to get out of here?"

"Have we been released already?" I asked him, surprised by the chief's quick action. "I haven't even been interviewed yet."

"I took care of that for you, since you never left my side the entire time we've been here," he said.

"Where do things stand right now?" I asked, not willing to leave the estate just yet.

"The chief took everything I said under advisement, and he

reserved the right to call on me later if he needs me, but for now, he's handling things on his own."

"Did he say anything more about your theory on what happened?" I asked.

"He's still willing to consider it, and really, that's all that I can expect him to do. After all, it's his investigation, not mine. Now come on. I don't want to hang around here any longer than I have to."

"Can we make one more stop before we leave the house?" I asked.

Jake frowned. "Suzanne, there's no way the chief is going to give you another peek at the crime scene, so do us all a favor and don't even ask."

"That wasn't my request. I'd like to stop by the kitchen and find out what's going to happen to all of that food," I answered. "I suggested it be donated to the soup kitchen, but I'm not at all sure that Bethesda took it seriously."

"I suppose that's a legitimate line of inquiry," he said. "Chief Grant shouldn't have a problem with that."

"Does that mean that he has issues with us investigating Jasper's murder?" I asked him.

"The truth is, he's not crazy about it," Jake said with a shrug, "but he's not exactly barring the behavior either, at least not yet."

"But he might at some point in the future. Is that what you're saying?" I asked him.

"I don't know. Jasper Finney's murder is a high-profile case. Ray Blake isn't going to be the only newsman sniffing around here, and the chief understandably doesn't want to deal with any outside interference that he doesn't have to." I grinned at my husband upon hearing that, and Jake asked me, "Did I just say something funny?"

"I don't think I've ever been called an outside interference before."

"To your face, you mean?" Jake asked with a smile.

"To my face," I agreed. "Come on. Let's stop by the kitchen, and then we'll go home and get something good to eat. It's a shame we can't take some of the DeAngelis food with us."

"Maybe we should ask," Jake said with a grin. "I just hate seeing anything go to waste."

"It won't," I answered. "If it's going to the soup kitchen, we can't very well lighten the load, now can we?"

"Not even if we make a sizeable donation instead?" Jake asked, only half kidding unless I missed my guess.

"Not even then. Don't worry. I'll feed you when we get home."

"Maybe we should go to the Boxcar instead," Jake suggested.

"Do you suddenly have a problem with my cooking?" I asked him as I stopped in my tracks.

"What? No! Of course not! I'm just thinking that if Trish is shutting the place down soon, we should take advantage of her being there while we still can. Besides, aren't you curious about where things stand with her?"

"Yes, absolutely. Nice save, by the way," I said with a smile as we headed for the kitchen.

I happened to glance out the window on our way, and I caught sight of someone skulking in the bushes. It was Bobby Finney!

What on earth was he up to?

CHAPTER 10

"WHAT ARE YOU DOING OUT there, Bobby?" I called out to him as I threw the window open.

He looked startled to see Jake and me standing there watching him. "I dropped my wallet earlier," he said lamely. It was clearly the first thing that had popped into his head, and I doubted there was the slightest chance that it was true.

"Hang on. We'll come right out and help you look," I said.

"Thanks, but that's okay. I don't need any help," he offered lamely.

"Nonsense. We'll be out in a second." I turned to Jake and said softly, "Watch him while I go out to see him."

"What am I supposed to be looking for?" Jake asked, clearly curious about what I had in mind.

"I want to see if he 'mysteriously' finds his wallet after all," I said as I headed for the nearest door.

As I made my way toward Bobby, once I was outside, he waved something in the air. "You must be my good luck charm, Suzanne. The second you offered to help, I found it."

"What a happy coincidence," I said as I glanced back at the house. I couldn't see Jake from where we were standing, but I did see something else of interest.

From Bobby Finney's vantage point, I could see straight into Jasper's study and the busy ongoing investigation still going on there.

"I'll walk you back in," I offered, suspecting what he was going to say.

"No, that's okay. I need some air anyway. Thanks for offering, though."

"You're most welcome," I said as I returned inside and found Jake waiting for me at the door. "Well? What did you see?"

"You were right. The second you vanished, he pulled his wallet from his back pocket and let it slip to the ground. After a moment, he reached down, retrieved it, and waved it in the air as you approached him. How did you know he was going to do that?"

"I didn't, at least not with any certainty, but I had a suspicion. Guess what I saw when I was outside?"

"I don't even know where to begin to start guessing," my husband said, and then, before I could tell him, he held up a hand and grinned. "He was watching the ongoing investigation in Jasper's study, wasn't he?"

"Excellent. That's one gold star for you," I told him.

"What could he possibly have been hoping to see?" Jake asked me as we resumed our trek to the kitchen.

"That's the question, isn't it?"

"One of many," my husband agreed.

We arrived at the kitchen to find Bethesda packing up not only the DeAngelis food but my donuts as well. "A truck is just pulling up. The soup kitchen was thrilled with the donation. Thank you for the suggestion, Suzanne."

"Hey, it belonged to the estate after I got paid," I said, "but for what it's worth, I'm happy to know that it's all going to a good cause."

"As am I. After my father died when I was a little girl, we didn't have a great deal, so my mother depended on the soup kitchen to feed us all."

"How did your dad die?" I asked.

"They said that it was an industrial accident, but my mother was never satisfied that she ever got the entire story," Bethesda said, and from the troubled expression on her face, I knew that I shouldn't push her any harder about it.

"I'm so sorry," I said. "I lost my father, too." I looked around at the food, and I asked her, "Is there anything we can do to help?"

"No, they promised to send a full crew to collect all of this, but thank you for asking."

I was about to follow up with a question about when she'd last seen Jasper Finney when Chief Grant came into the kitchen. "Is there any coffee left back here?" he asked, and then he spotted us. "What are you two still doing here?"

"We're seeing about the fate of the donuts and the other food provided," I said, not wanting to admit that I had more motivation than that in mind for lingering at the crime scene.

"I understood that it was already being taken care of," he said as he looked at Bethesda.

"It has been," she said simply.

"Then there's no reason for you to hang around," the chief said.

"Are you trying to get rid of us, Chief?" I asked him.

"Not you specifically, but there are entirely too many people on this estate that don't need to be here at the moment."

"Does that include Jasper's family, and his former partner, too?" I asked.

"No. They're all staying here, at my request, for at least the next forty-eight hours. After that, I'm not sure what's going to happen."

"Don't worry. You'll solve it in time," Jake said as he patted the chief on the shoulder.

"It remains to be seen whether that's true or not," he said. "I'll talk to you both later," he added.

Jake and I had no choice at that point. Not only had we run out of opportunities to question my suspects, but we'd also been personally asked to leave the scene of the crime by the investigating officer. Things didn't get more emphatic than that.

I decided to smile and joke my way out. "Chief, I can take a hint. After all, I've been thrown out of nicer places than this before."

"And no doubt you will be again if history repeats itself," he said with a smile.

It proved that we were still on good terms with the chief, something that was extremely important to me. Not only was he romantically linked to my best friend, Grace, but we were also friends in our own right, not to mention the close relationship he had with Jake.

I didn't want to vex him with my investigation if I could help it.

I just wasn't entirely certain that I'd be able to prevent it moving forward.

"We need to stop off at the donut shop on our way to the Boxcar Grill," I told Jake as we approached my business.

"What's wrong? Did you forget to turn the fryer off or something?" he asked with a smile.

"Don't even tease about that. At the worst, it might burn the place down, but even if nothing catastrophic happened, the gas bill would be too painful to bear."

"Sorry. Seriously though, what did you forget?"

"Do you remember the envelope Jasper gave me yesterday?" I asked him as he pulled the truck into a spot up front. "I told you about it last night."

"Sure. I remember," he said, his voice wavering a bit as he spoke.

"Tell the truth," I pushed him.

"It might have slipped past me, but in my defense, I'd had a long day. What was in it?"

"That's what I mean to find out," I said as I unlocked the door and walked into the donut shop.

As he followed me inside, my husband asked me, "Are you telling me that you didn't even open it?"

"No. He asked me not to until the day he died. The truth is, I thought I'd have a lot more time before I had to read it. Jake, is it possible that Jasper had some kind of inkling that he was about to be murdered?" I asked him as I searched for my apron. Where was it? I distinctly remembered throwing it on the counter as I was leaving, but it wasn't there.

"Suzanne, Jasper gathered together three family members who didn't care for him and a partner who threatened to kill him on multiple occasions. I don't think it took any clairvoyance on his part to figure out that he might not make it through the night."

"Maybe not, but I still want to see what he wrote," I said. Could I have put it on my desk in back without realizing what I was doing? I had been preoccupied with completing the extra donut order. Maybe I was slipping. "It's not here, either," I said after I checked and failed yet again to find it.

"The letter?" Jake asked.

"Yes, but my apron's gone, too. Jake, somebody broke in here and stole them both."

"Hang on. Let's not jump to any conclusions just yet," Jake said. "Let's look at this rationally."

"How am I not doing that now? I'm positive I left my apron here when we left after loading up the donuts, and yet now it has vanished, including the letter Jasper wrote me tucked into one of the pockets. How much more logical than that do I need to be?"

Jake shrugged as he moved to the front door again. After examining it closely, he frowned at me and said, "There's no sign of tampering."

"Could the thief have broken in without you seeing any traces of what he'd done?" I asked. After all, it happened enough in the mysteries I read with my book club.

"That's just fiction," Jake answered. "It would take a world-class locksmith to break into this place without leaving some sign of it behind. Besides, picking a lock isn't as easy as it looks in the movies."

"Have you ever picked one yourself?" I asked him.

He nodded as he admitted grudgingly, "We were taught how to do it at the academy."

"Did you ever use it in the field?"

Instead of answering me directly, Jake just shrugged. When he didn't add any further details, I thought about pushing him, but Jake could be surprisingly reticent at times about his past in law enforcement.

"So, whoever stole it must have had access to a key," I said.

"Call Emma," he told me. "Maybe she knows what's going on."

I dialed her number, but it went straight to voicemail. Then I called her parents' house to see where she might be. That letter could be extremely important in finding out who had killed Jasper, and I wasn't about to rest until I knew where it was.

"Hey, Sharon," I said when Emma's mother answered. I was more than a little relieved that it hadn't been Ray. I would give him the promised report eventually, and the photos Jake had taken as well, but I didn't want to deal with the newspaperman at the moment. "Is Emma around, by any chance?"

"No, she's off with Barton," Sharon said. "I don't know when she'll be back. Did you try calling her on her cell phone?"

"It went straight to voicemail," I admitted.

"Well, the two of them probably didn't even hear it ringing. They've been working every spare hour they can find planning Barton's pop-up restaurant."

"What do you think about their relationship?" I asked her. It might have been a nosy question coming from someone else—actually it was nosy coming from me—but I wanted to know what Sharon thought.

"I think they're good for each other," Sharon said. "What do you think?" she asked me in return.

"I agree with you," I said.

"Good. I'm sure Emma will be relieved to learn that we both approve," Sharon replied. Before I could protest that might not be the best idea telling her, she added, "I'm just kidding, Suzanne. I'm not entirely sure that either of our opinions matter, so I'm doing my best to stay out of it and let them find their own way."

"That sounds like a solid plan to me," I said. "Listen, could you have her call me when she gets in? It doesn't matter what time it is."

"Is something wrong?" Sharon asked, her voice suddenly filled with concern.

"I just need to ask her something, but it can wait," I replied. There was no use involving more people in my quest than I had to.

"Okay then. I'll leave her a note, but there's no guarantee that she'll see it."

"I appreciate it," I said, and then I hung up. "Sharon said that Emma was with Barton."

"Did I just hear you two discussing that poor girl's relationship?" Jake asked me.

"I was just curious about what she thought of it," I admitted.

"I take it you both approve," Jake replied.

"Yes, but we're not telling Emma that," I said as I started searching the donut shop again. It was amazing how many places the apron *wasn't* as I looked, and Jake even pitched in himself.

"That's odd," he said after we'd concluded that the apron was gone.

"What's that?"

"Shouldn't Emma's apron be here, too?" he asked me.

It hadn't even occurred to me that hers was missing as well. So was Sharon's for that matter. "Do we have an apron thief on our hands?" I asked him.

"It appears so," Jake said. "Searching the place again isn't going to do us any good. Don't worry. I'm sure we'll crack the case and solve the mystery sooner or later."

"I hope you're right," I said. "Let's lock up and head home."

"You mean the Boxcar Grill, right?" Jake reminded me.

In my frantic search for my apron, I'd forgotten all about our plans to eat at the grill and speak with Trish about her lottery ticket dilemma. "That's exactly what I mean. Let's just leave the truck here and walk across the street," I suggested.

"Sounds good to me. That will give me a chance to work up an appetite."

I laughed at my husband's suggestion. "It's not that far a walk, you know."

"Hey, every step counts," he replied.

The diner was half full when we walked in, and Trish sported a frown, at least until she saw us. "Come on in. Pick any seat."

"What happened to the crowd of customers you had before?" I asked her.

"Once they found out that I wasn't giving food away anymore, they seemed to have all lost interest," she answered.

"Any word on the ticket status yet?" I asked her.

"Your mom's attorney is coming by tomorrow to talk to me," Trish said. "I'm beginning to think I should give it back to its rightful owner, no matter what the lawyer says."

"Why would you do that?" Jake asked. "It was your tip, so I'd think that would make it yours."

"If he really meant to leave it at all," Trish said. "I'm just not sure I want something not willingly given to me, you know?"

"I get that, but don't make any decisions until you speak with the attorney," I said. "What's the special tonight?"

"Hilda and Gladys aren't too happy with me, as you might imagine. They've both suddenly realized that they may be out of work if this win is real. Why that didn't occur to them before is beyond me, but what are you going to do?" Trish asked, naming the two women who did the majority of the cooking at the Boxcar Grill. Though they were rarely seen by the customers, I knew firsthand how important they both were to the place's well-being. "The truth is, they made a noxious stew that people keep sending back. If I were you, I'd stick with burgers and fries. Those should at least be safe."

"Consider our arms twisted. We'll have burgers and fries," Jake said. "Don't worry. They'll come around."

"I hope so," Trish said.

Jake and I found a table, and soon our food was delivered.

"Should we trust these?" I asked Trish as she delivered our plates.

"I told them it was for you, so you should be fine," Trish said. "I, on the other hand, will be eating at home until this is resolved. I'm not saying that they'd poison me, but why take the chance?" She grinned as she said it, but I had to wonder just how badly the cooks were taking the news that she might be shutting the place down.

After we'd had a few bites, I looked at Jake and asked softly, "Is it me, or is this lacking something?"

"It's not just you," he agreed. "The cooks may claim they are fine with us, but I'm not so sure. Should we just leave it and eat at home after all?"

"No, I don't want to hurt Trish's feelings," I said as I handed him the catsup bottle. "Soldier on."

"I will if you will," Jake said. He poured a healthy amount of catsup onto his plate, and then he handed the bottle back to me. I drowned my burger and fries in the catsup, and we both managed to get through most of the meal. In all honesty, it was probably on par with most fast food restaurants, but I held the Boxcar Grill to a higher standard than that. I hoped Trish had the ticket issue settled one way or another soon, or Jake and I were going to have to start eating at home more.

CHAPTER 11

As I WAS GETTING OUT of Jake's truck back at the cottage, my cell phone began to ring. Hoping it was Emma, I grabbed it without even checking the caller ID.

That turned out to be a mistake.

"Suzanne, why haven't you called me?" Ray Blake asked angrily the moment after I answered.

"Things have been kind of crazy, as I'm sure you can understand," I said. "I'm assuming you heard what happened to Jasper?"

"Of course I heard. Please tell me that you at least got a shot of the crime scene."

"I tried, but my hands might have been shaking. I can't make any promises," I said as Jake started grinning.

"No matter. I'll be over in four minutes to get my camera," Ray said, and then he hung up on me before I had a chance to protest his visiting us.

"He's coming over," I said as I put my phone away.

"Here? Now?" Jake asked, clearly unhappy about the newspaperman's plan as well.

"Sorry. I tried to stop him, but he hung up on me before I could tell him not to come."

"Let's go inside," Jake said as he rushed for the door.

"What are we going to do, barricade ourselves in?" I asked him as I trotted behind him.

"That's a thought, but I want to download those shots

onto my computer and delete anything that might hurt Jasper's memory before Ray gets here," he said.

"That's sweet of you, but he's long past caring now," I told him.

"Still, we owe him at least that much," Jake said as he pulled out his laptop and started it up. As he scanned through the photos he'd taken while he was waiting, I said, "You're going to copy those to your computer, right?"

"You bet I am," Jake said. My husband was pretty tech savvy, even more so than I was, so I was glad he was handling that.

"Is there anything we need to delete?" I asked as we looked at the pictures en masse.

"No, these all look fairly harmless to me," he said. After Jake finished loading the images in question, he pulled the card out of his computer reader and slapped it back into the camera.

"Just in time, too," I said as I heard a car pull up outside. "Let me have it."

"I'm not even sure we should give it back to him," Jake said with a frown.

"We don't have much choice. An agreement is an agreement," I said. "Besides, he gave me some useful information earlier about Jasper's family and friends."

"If you can call them that," Jake said.

Ray started pounding on the door and ringing the bell at the same time. I expected my husband to blow up, but instead, he was smiling. "What's so funny?"

"I say we let him wear himself out before we answer the door," Jake replied.

"I would, but I'm already starting to get a headache from all of the noise." I walked to the door, but before I opened it, in an impish moment I called out, "Who is it?"

"Suzanne Hart, you know full well who it is," Ray said heatedly. "Open this blasted door and let me in this instant!"

Jake gently moved me aside, and then he opened the door himself. "Ray, you need to take a breath and settle down before you say something you're going to regret," Jake said in a soft voice that was scary nonetheless.

"Sorry," Ray said, doing an immediate turnabout. "Do you have my camera?" he asked gently as he held out his hand.

I gave it to him. "Like I said, don't expect much. Things were kind of crazy this afternoon."

"Did you at least get a shot of the body?" he asked, fairly panting in anticipation of my response.

I had, but not with his camera. "Sorry. I don't think so. There wasn't much time, you see. We were thrown out almost as soon as we found him," I said, which wasn't completely true.

"I understand," Ray said, though his expression showed that he was clearly unhappy with the news. "Tell me about it."

"Ray, can't this wait until tomorrow?" Jake asked.

"Sorry, but I'm running a special edition in the morning. As it is, I'll be up all night putting it together." It was clear that this was one of those situations the man lived for despite his protests to the contrary.

"It's all right. We can take a minute and tell him what happened," I told Jake.

"Okay, but you've got four minutes, and not a second more," my husband told Ray.

The newspaperman was about to protest, but he must have read my husband's body language, because he quickly agreed to the new conditions.

We all moved into the living room, but I didn't offer the newsman coffee, or any other beverage, for that matter. This wasn't a social call. Ray took out a tape recorder, and to my surprise, Jake produced one himself.

"Are you taping this, too?" Ray asked him, clearly not happy about seeing another recorder besides the one he'd brought.

"I just want to be sure that there's no confusion later about what is being said here tonight," Jake said. "You don't mind, do you?"

It was clear the journalist would have rather eaten a live worm, but he reluctantly nodded in agreement. "I wouldn't have it any other way."

Jake and I told our stories, hitting just the highlighted facts and including absolutely none of our speculations. Ray kept probing us for more details, but Jake and I held firm to our bare-minimalist retelling. After being asked the same leading questions three different ways, Jake stood, shut off his recorder, and said, "That's it. Time's up."

Ray glanced at his watch. "But I have one more minute."

"Then ask us an original question," Jake said as he turned his recorder back on.

"Who do you think killed Jasper Finney?"

"We don't know," Jake said abruptly.

"Suzanne? Surely you must have a theory of your own."

I didn't, at least not yet, but I wasn't about to admit it. "Sorry. I can't help you."

"Are you telling me that you're not going to investigate this murder on your own?" Ray asked. He then kept his mouth shut, waiting for me to reply.

I knew that trick though. I didn't even shake my head. I just sat there until Jake announced, "And now your time is officially up."

"Thanks for everything," Ray said, though he didn't sound very sincere at all.

"Hey, a deal's a deal," I said. "Do you happen to know where Emma is right now?"

"With that chef kid," Ray replied. It was obvious that he didn't share his wife's view of their daughter's relationship.

"Don't you care for Barton?" I asked him, honestly curious about it.

"He's okay, I guess," Ray said as he put his recorder away and headed for the door. "If your dad was still around, he'd tell you the same thing. No man ever born would be good enough for his daughter."

"I don't know. I have a hunch that he would have approved of Jake," I said.

"You never know," Ray said with a shrug. "Maybe you're right."

As the newspaperman headed for the door, Jake surprised me by saying, "You should give him a chance. He's a good guy."

"Yeah, I probably should, but I don't know if I can," Ray said with a shrug.

"She could do much worse, you know," I added.

"That's what keeps me awake at night. Thanks again," Ray said, and then he finally left.

It had been a long day, and a double shift at that, so sleep wasn't that far off for me. Besides, I had a big day tomorrow.

I might not be making any donuts, but I was going to try to solve my friend's murder, and that was going to be a daunting task in and of itself.

Jake came into the kitchen the next morning a little after seven. I'd gotten better at sleeping in on my days off, but I was still up well before six. My husband had always been an early riser as well, but for some reason, he'd slept in this morning.

"Hey. Been up long?" he asked me as he rubbed his cheek with one hand.

"Not long," I said as I kissed him good morning. "I made you some bacon, and I can whip you up some eggs in a heartbeat if you'd like me to."

"That sounds wonderful," Jake said as he poured himself

some coffee. "Have I told you lately how much I enjoy you taking two days off every week?"

"As a matter of fact, you have, repeatedly," I said with a grin as I got his eggs started. "Are you still going back to Hickory this morning?"

"I don't have much choice. They need me," he acknowledged. "Any chance you'll come with me?"

We'd discussed that as a possibility earlier, but that had been before Jasper had been murdered. That event had changed everything, as far as I was concerned.

"Sorry, I can't. I'm going back out to the estate," I said.

"I can probably cancel if you'd like me to go with you," Jake offered.

"No, you need to tie up all of those loose ends there. I'll be okay on my own," I said as I finished scrambling his eggs. As they finished cooking, I crumbled up three of the bacon slices, and after I added that to the mix, I threw in a little shredded cheese, too. I liked my eggs a different way entirely, but I was happy to be able to make Jake his own style of breakfast whenever I had the chance.

"Am I just wasting my breath if I tell you that I don't like you going out there by yourself?" he asked as the toast popped up and he grabbed it. Jake slathered on a hearty coating of butter, much more than I would have given him, which was probably one of the reasons he'd done it himself.

"I'll be fine. No one's going to try anything in broad daylight."

"I've heard that before, and yet it's happened on occasion, hasn't it?" he asked. "The bad guys don't just operate at night."

"If I call Grace, will that make you feel better?"

"Yes, strangely enough, somehow it would," he admitted. "The two of you manage to generate together more than double the trouble you get yourselves into, but you also seem to get out of it, too."

"So far, at any rate." I grinned at him, holding up two sets of crossed fingers.

"Just call her, smarty pants," Jake prodded me.

"I'll do it while you're in the shower," I promised. "If I know her, she's not even up yet, so I'm going to let her sleep as long as I can."

"I don't know how she does it," Jake said. "I'd be groggy all day long if I slept that late."

"Hey, she's improved a lot since high school. I used to have to go over and douse her with cold water every other day to get her to classes on time."

"You're a true friend, Suzanne. Hey, that looks perfect," he added as I plated the scrambled egg concoction and slid it in front of him.

"I hope you like it."

Jake took a bite, and then he grinned widely. "It's perfect. Any chance I can get you to make this for me every morning? My version doesn't taste nearly as good as yours does."

"Why? Because it's made with love?" I asked him.

"No, that's not it. I always manage to burn the eggs when I try it," he said with a grin.

I kept my husband company as he ate, and after he was finished and in the shower, I dialed Grace's number. I'd been expecting to wake her, but to my surprise, she sounded as though she'd been up for hours. "Hey, Suzanne. What's up?"

"You're awake," I said, almost accusingly.

"I know. Can you believe it?" she asked, and I could hear the grin in her voice. "I was all set for the sleepover at Jasper's last night, but when that didn't happen, I figured I'd take the day off and hang out with you. Minerva had different thoughts on the matter, though."

"Minerva? Who is that?"

"She's my new sales rep," Grace said. "At least she was. She started working in her territory four days ago, and she just quit."

"Wow, that's fast, even for you," I said. "What happened?"

"That's what I'm going to find out. We invested money in training her for a month, and I'm not going to let it go to waste without a better answer than she's given me so far. I hope you don't mind that I'm not going to be there for you this morning."

"I can hardly resent the fact that you're off doing your job," I said. It might interfere with my promise to Jake, but I couldn't expect Grace to always drop everything just because I was digging into another murder.

"I know. Who ever would have dreamed that I'd be so conscientious?" she asked with a laugh.

"I don't know. I always had a hunch," I said with the hint of a smile in my voice.

"That makes one of us, anyway. Are you going to be okay without me?" she asked.

"I'll manage, as difficult as it might be," I replied with a laugh of my own. "Call me when you get back into town."

"At least you've got Jake, right?" she asked me.

"Right," I said. There was no way I was going to guilt her into not doing her job just because it meant that I'd be going solo. "I'll talk to you this afternoon."

"See you later, alligator," she said as she signed off.

Jake came out, buttoning his shirt. "That was fast, even for you," I said.

"What can I say? I was motivated to get going this morning. Is Grace going with you?"

"She has to take care of a few things with her job first, but after that, she's all mine," I said. I'd briefly considered shading the truth a little with Jake, but in the end, I knew that I wouldn't be happy with myself if I did that. I'd rather take his consternation now than have him be disappointed in me later when he found out the truth.

"But you're going anyway, aren't you?" he asked me with a frown.

"Come on. I won't go into any dark corners, and I won't even ask any probing questions. I just want to see if I can figure out what happened to Jasper."

My husband seemed to think about that for a few seconds before he answered. "If you aren't going to ask questions or look into blind alleys, what's the point of going? Hey, there's something I forgot to tell you last night."

"What's that?"

"I checked out the lock to the study after you went off on your own yesterday," he said.

"Did you find something wrong with it?"

"No, but the only way to lock it is with a key, whether you're on the inside or the outside of the door. Whoever left Jasper for dead had to have had a key themselves."

"Or they knew where to get their hands on one," I said as I kissed his cheek. "Thanks for worrying about me. It's nice having someone in my life who cares about my well-being."

"You have more folks than me doing that. I still don't want you going alone, though. Why don't you call your mother?"

"Seriously? I'm a grown woman, Jake. I can do this on my own," I said, adding a little spirit to my voice. I enjoyed the fact that he cared about me, but I was also not afraid of doing things by myself, and he needed to accept that as being a part of me.

"Sorry. I get it," he said, holding his hands up in surrender and taking a step backward.

Now I'd gone too far. I softened my tone as I explained, "I'll be careful. I promise. Now don't you need to go? I don't want you being late on my account."

"We couldn't have that, could we?" he asked, lightening up a little. "At least tell me you've got a full charge on your phone battery."

I pulled it out and checked it, only to find that the battery was down to fifteen percent. "I'll charge it in the Jeep as I drive," I promised.

"You're trying to give me a heart attack, aren't you?" he asked me with a grin.

"Anything but," I said. "Now shoo. We both need to get out of here."

"Call me whenever you get a chance," he said as he grabbed his wallet and keys.

"Will you honestly be able to take my phone calls if I do?" I asked him.

"No, probably not," he admitted. "But if you get into anything you're not comfortable with, at least call Chief Grant. If you promise me you'll keep the police chief informed, I'll go and try not to worry about you too much today."

"And if I don't?" I asked him.

"Then I'm cancelling my day and I'm going to shadow you," he said. There was no doubt in my mind that he was telling the truth.

"Fine. I'll call the chief at the first hint of trouble," I promised him.

"Good enough. I'll walk you out," he said.

Jake got into his truck, and I slid into my Jeep's driver's seat. I hadn't heard from Emma yet that morning in response to my query the night before, so I wouldn't be driving behind him for long. I was planning to stop at the donut shop on my way to the Finney estate. Hopefully Emma had seen my apron, as well as the letter in its pocket, but if not, I'd still grab a dozen donuts and take them with me as an icebreaker. I'd learned long ago that donuts could get me a lot more mileage than mere smiles could manage, and I aimed to take advantage of that fact.

CHAPTER 12

"I THOUGHT YOU WERE OFF TODAY," Emma said with a frown when I walked into Donut Hearts. The place was hopping, which wasn't that much of a surprise, given the time of morning. "You're not checking up on me, are you?"

"I wouldn't dream of it," I said. "We do have a problem, though."

Emma's face clouded up. Sometimes I forgot that she was barely into her twenties. It seemed as though we'd been friends, not just coworkers, forever. "Oh crud. I didn't call you back. It was late when I got your message, but that's no excuse. Suzanne, please don't fire me."

"Emma, I would *never* fire you," I said, concerned about her sudden worry about her job security.

"Never?" she asked me with the hint of a smile.

"Well, *almost* never, but I wouldn't push that too much, if I were you," I said.

"I really am sorry," Emma said. "What did you want?"

"I was wondering if you'd seen my apron," I said. "I thought for sure I left it on the counter when we left, but I came back later and couldn't find it."

"That's because I took it when I came back after I went to the bank," she said with a frown. "I like to take our aprons home and have my mother wash them before we start our two days a week running the shop. I hope you don't mind, but I always throw yours in, too."

"Of course I don't mind. In fact, I appreciate it. I was just hoping to find something in the pocket I'd left behind," I said.

"Do you mean this?" Emma asked as she opened the register and pulled out the letter Jasper had given me earlier.

"That's exactly what I was looking for. Was it in there the entire time?"

She nodded. "I thought it might be important, so I stuck it there until I could give it to you myself. Are you sure I'm not in trouble?"

"For doing me a favor? What kind of boss would I be if I punished you for that?" I asked her, and then I gave her a quick hug. "How's it going?"

"Great," she said. "Mom's in back doing the dishes, and I'm taking care of the front."

I surveyed the donuts in the case, and I saw that she had a healthy inventory for the time of morning. "Mind if I take a dozen with me?"

"Hey, it's your donut shop. You can clean me out if you'd like. That way we can close up and go home, so go right ahead. You have my blessing."

"I just need a dozen," I said with a smile. After I folded up a box and filled it with a nice variety of goodies, I closed the lid and handed her a ten.

"You know you don't have to pay for your own donuts, don't you?" Emma asked.

"I know, but I don't want to throw your report off, either."

My assistant shrugged as she made change for me, but she didn't say a word about my behavior. I was dying to read that letter, but I wasn't going to do it in front of the prying eyes of some of the town. I noticed that several customers were feigning interest in their donuts as they watched us and listening in as well. "Has anybody been talking about what happened to Jasper?" I asked her softly.

"Are you kidding? That's the only topic of conversation around here this morning."

"What's the consensus, or is there one?" I asked.

"Half the town thinks someone in his family did it, and the other half think it was someone from his past in business," she admitted. "When he shut that factory down, a lot of people lost their jobs."

"Perfect. That does me absolutely no good at all," I said with a smile.

"Glad to be of service, ma'am," she said. "Now, if there's nothing else, I've got donuts to sell."

"Don't let me get in your way," I replied.

I was just turning to leave when someone very familiar stepped into Donut Hearts.

It was my stepfather and the former chief of police, Phillip Martin.

"I thought you were off today," he told me in an almost accusatory voice.

"That's the second time this morning someone has asked me that exact same question," I said. "I didn't realize folks were keeping so close a track on my schedule."

"I didn't mean anything by it," Phillip said reluctantly. "Do me a favor, though. Don't tell your mother you saw me here."

"Why shouldn't I? Phillip, are you doing something you shouldn't be doing?" There was no way this man was cheating on my mother. He was as devoted a husband to her as Jake was to me.

But that didn't mean that he wasn't up to something, either.

"I'm not strictly supposed to have donuts," he admitted.

"Your mother is gone for the day, though, and I knew you weren't working, so I figured what would it hurt?" He asked the last bit with a tragic grin, and I knew I wouldn't be able to rat him out to my mother unless she asked me a direct question about it. The man had certainly grown on me since becoming a part of our family; that much was undeniable.

"How about this? I won't volunteer the information, but if she asks me a direct question, I won't lie to her. How does that sound to you?" I asked him.

"That works for me," he answered happily. "After all, all I'm asking for is a fighting chance." He tapped the box of donuts in my hand. "It appears I'm not the only one feeling a little peckish today."

"These aren't for me," I said.

"Sure, and the three I'm about to get aren't for me, either," he answered with a smile. "I won't judge you if you don't judge me."

"Actually, I'm taking them out to the Finney estate," I admitted softly.

Phillip looked around. "By yourself?" He must have seen storm clouds arriving on my face, because he quickly added, "Not that there's anything wrong with that. It's just that you usually investigate these things with Jake or Grace."

"They were both tied up," I admitted.

"Well, I'm free. How about if I go with you?" he offered.

"Do you honestly think I need a babysitter, too?" I asked him. "And be very careful how you answer that."

"Heck, I need something to do, and digging into a current murder sounds like fun to me. Besides, cops have partners and backup for a reason, Suzanne." My stepfather enjoyed solving crimes, but usually he restricted his investigations to long-dead cases from the past. "What do you say?"

"I say grab your donuts and let's go," I said. At least it would make Jake happy, and Momma too, most likely. Besides,

I wouldn't mind having him with me, either. After all, being stubborn made perfect sense sometimes, but then again, so did being prudent when the occasion called for it.

"You're on," he said. "I'll even let you drive."

"Why is that? So you can eat while I chauffeur us to the house?" I asked him.

"You bet, and what's more, I'm not even ashamed to admit it," he said. "Just give me a minute to order, and I'll be right out and join you in the Jeep."

"Take your time," I said. I carried my donuts out of the shop, stowed them in the back seat, and then I pulled out the letter Jasper had given me, leaning against my car door. My name was written in his distinctive handwriting, and I found myself missing my friend yet again.

But this wasn't an opportunity for sentimentality.

It was time to find out exactly what Jasper had wanted to tell me from beyond the grave.

To my surprise, a single, crisp, one-hundred-dollar bill fluttered out of the envelope, along with a letter as well. I caught the errant bill and tucked it back into the envelope as I looked around. No one had seen it, at least as far as I could tell. Why would Jasper give me money? It didn't take long to understand his rationale after I read the brief note inside, though, also written in his fine hand.

> *Dear Suzanne,*
>
> *I know this may sound a bit morbid to you, but I'd love it if you'd bring lots of your delicious donuts to my place when folks get together to say good-bye after I die. Your treats have always cheered me up while I've been alive, and I can't think of a more*

fitting tribute than to provide them for my family and friends one last time after I'm gone.

Your friend,
Jasper.

So, it wasn't a dying clue after all. I'd been hoping that Jasper had some inkling as to who might have wanted to kill him, but if he did, the man didn't choose to share that information with me.

If I was going to have any luck solving his murder, I was going to have to do it without any help from the murder victim.

CHAPTER 13

"WHAT DO YOU HAVE THERE?" Phillip asked me as he rejoined me outside. I'd called Emma as soon as I'd read it, not wanting to tell the entire world what we were doing face to face. This was private, between Jasper and us, and I wanted to keep it that way. Fortunately she was able to help me, so we made arrangements to meet back at Donut Hearts after lunch in order to make more donuts yet again.

"It's a letter from Jasper," I said.

My stepfather looked at me skeptically before replying. "Do you want to tell me about it?"

"It's simple, really. He gave it to me the day before he died," I said. "It's a request for me to provide donuts at his wake, or viewing, or whatever you want to call it. He even paid me in advance."

"That sounds as though it was an act of a man who knew that he was about to die," Phillip said after pausing a moment. "I wish he'd given you a list of folks he suspected in his murder instead of placing a donut order from beyond the grave."

"Me, too, but what can we do about it? He didn't. Are you ready to go?"

"I am," he said, and we both got into my Jeep.

"Do I need to wait to start driving until you're finished eating?"

"No, you go right ahead. I'm good at multitasking," he said.

"I showed a little restraint and only got two donuts instead of three."

"Wow, you're a marvel at self-control," I said with a grin.

"I know. I should go back and reward myself with a third donut, shouldn't I?" he asked with a tilted grin.

"Let's put a pin in that for now and head over to the Finney place," I said as I started the Jeep and drove off.

"Spoilsport," he said good-naturedly.

"You know it," I said.

Phillip was finished before we got to the Finney estate, which was due more to his eating pace than my driving. As I pulled into the parking area, he asked, "Who are we going to tackle first?"

"Let's drop off the donuts and see if anyone's hanging around the kitchen," I suggested as we both got out and moved toward the house.

"That sounds like a plan to me," he said. "You lead, and I'll follow."

"On the walk to the house, or the investigation?" I asked him with a smile.

"Both are fine with me. Don't mind me. I'm just here for backup."

"You know," I said as we started walking, "I like you a lot better since you retired. No offense intended."

"None taken," he said with a grin. "I like you better too, since we're not butting heads anymore. I'd rather be on your side than against you, and I've got to admit, you've gotten pretty good at investigating over the years."

"I'll take that as a compliment," I said.

"That's certainly the way I meant it."

We got to the house, and Phillip looked expectantly at me for a cue as to what we should do next. "Should we knock first, or just barge on in?"

"I think I'd feel better if we knocked," I admitted.

He dutifully rapped on the door a few times and then rang the bell, too, for good measure.

Ethan opened the door, and he didn't look one bit pleased to see us. "Were we expecting you?" he asked archly.

"No, but I thought I'd make a donut delivery," I said cheerfully as I held them up.

"That's thoughtful of you," Ethan said as he started to take them.

I wasn't going to let that happen, though. Without that box of donuts, I wasn't going to get in the door, and I had other plans besides being a breakfast delivery person. "Why don't I take them in for you? They're delicate, and I'd hate to see some of the icing smudged. Besides, we need to discuss something else that's just come up."

Ethan looked at me oddly, but then he stepped aside. "This is my stepfather," I said, introducing Phillip in as innocent a way as I could manage. I wasn't about to go out of my way to tell anyone there who didn't already know it that Phillip was the former police chief. After all, there was no reason to raise anyone's suspicions if I could help it.

"You were the sheriff around here once, weren't you?" Ethan asked with a hint of a frown.

It could have gone many ways, but to my delight, Phillip handled it perfectly. "Actually, I was the police chief, but that was a long time ago. I've been retired so long that sometimes it feels as though it was somebody else's life. I'm just hanging out with Suzanne today. I hope you don't mind." As he said the last bit, he walked into the house, leaving Ethan with little choice but to follow us both or stand there with the door open looking like a ninny.

He chose to follow us.

That meant that I had to go straight into the kitchen after

all, which was fine by me. "We were wondering if you were holding a wake," I said as we made our way to the kitchen.

"We are, but it's for family only. Sorry."

"That's fine," I said, "but Jasper asked me to provide donuts for you, so I need to know when and where to deliver them."

That stopped Ethan in his tracks. "When did my grandfather arrange for that to happen?"

"Oh, we were closer than you might have realized. In fact, he paid for them in advance, so we're all good on that front as well." I could have showed him his grandfather's letter, but he didn't even ask for proof that I was telling the truth.

"Very well," Ethan said. "You may bring them by the house this evening, but make it before six. After that, we're locking the doors and having a private celebration of his life before we open it to his friends in the community."

"I can do that," I said. At least I'd already warned Emma that we were pulling another double shift, but I didn't think she'd minded hearing the news. This time I was planning to give her *all* of the profits after my expenses. I just wouldn't feel right taking Jasper's money. This was something I wanted to do on my own to show my own respect to my friend.

"Do you have any idea who might have killed your grandfather?" I asked him as nonchalantly as I could manage it. It was something I'd learned a long time ago. Sometimes my suspects had the best clues to solving my cases if I only knew the right way to ask them.

"I have several, as a matter of fact. I don't seem to be able to think of anything else at the moment," he admitted.

"We'd love to hear your thoughts, if you wouldn't mind," Phillip said before I could jump in myself. "I knew Jasper for a long time. You might not realize it, but a great many folks in town are going to miss him."

"That news doesn't surprise me at all," he said with pursed lips.

"Who's at the top of your list?" I asked as we walked into the kitchen. Fortunately, it was deserted at the moment, so we could speak in private. There was a great deal of food already there, no doubt brought in by grieving friends, and unless I missed my guess, the refrigerator and freezer were probably at their bursting points as well.

"My cousin, Phyllis, is first on my list," he said softly. "She's run through quite a bit of money lately, especially since Henry came into her life. The only way out of the hole she's dug for herself is another inheritance."

"Do you know for sure that Jasper left his money to family?" I asked.

"As a matter of fact, I do. The attorney came by last night," Ethan said as he flipped the box open, selected a donut, and then took a bite. "The three of us are getting equal shares."

"Three?" I asked.

"Yes, Bobby is named to receive a full portion of the inheritance as well."

"How did Phyllis react to that news?" I asked.

"What do you mean?"

"I suspect she believed she'd be splitting it evenly with you," I admitted. "Isn't that what you thought yourself?"

"No, Jasper made it clear last week, at least to Bobby and me, that was what he was planning to do. I assumed he told Phyllis too, but from her reaction, that wasn't the case. She actually threatened to challenge the will, if you can imagine that."

"How did the attorney deal with that?" Phillip asked.

"He said that there was a provision in the will that stated that any challenges would disqualify the heir responsible for it instantly. That certainly settled that. Not that it matters any time soon."

"Why wouldn't it?" I asked him.

"Nothing will be distributed until Jasper's murderer has been tried and convicted of the crime," Ethan said.

"That seems reasonable enough to me," I said.

"Why is that?" Ethan asked. He was clearly unhappy about that particular twist. "It certainly penalizes those of us who didn't do it."

"A murderer can't profit from his crime," Phillip said.

"Then I sincerely hope that the chief finds the killer, and soon," Ethan said.

"Things are pretty tight for you too, aren't they?" I asked him gently. "Is there any way you can get a loan from the estate to carry you through until things are settled?"

He answered just before taking another bite. "No. I asked, but the attorney denied my request. You'd have thought Phyllis had won the lottery by the way she acted, but she won't get a dime until the murderer is caught either, so I don't quite know why she was celebrating." Ethan finished his donut, and then he said, "You've delivered your donuts, so it's time for you to leave. We have a great deal of family business to take care of before this evening. As I said before, we'll expect you before six, but not one minute after. Are we in agreement?"

"Yes, sir."

"Then it's time for you to go."

In ordinary circumstances, he would have been right, but I wasn't ready to leave just yet. I was trying to think of some kind of excuse I could use to linger when Phillip took care of it for me. "I hate to trouble you, but my new medications make me go to the bathroom every ten minutes. May I use your restroom? Otherwise I'll never make it back to town."

I didn't know if he was telling the truth, lying outright, or presenting a blend of both, but I didn't care as long as it got me what I wanted.

"Of course," Ethan said. "It's the fourth door on the right down the hallway."

If Jasper's grandson stayed with me, it wouldn't do me any good. I motioned my gaze toward the door, and Phillip picked up on it immediately. "I hate to play the part of the doddering old fool, but I get easily confused these days." That was a blatant lie, but Ethan seemed to accept it. "Could you show me the door yourself? Otherwise I'll never find it in time."

Ethan agreed reluctantly to the request and led Phillip away.

I had some time, but not much of it, and I planned to make the best of what I had.

I peeked my head out the door to make sure that Ethan had gone with Phillip when the man's son spotted me. "Playing hide and go seek, Suzanne?" he asked me with a grin. It was a little too cheerful for my taste, given the fact that his great-grandfather had just been murdered the day before.

"Actually, I was looking for you," I said. "I brought donuts."

"Cool. The only breakfast food around here has fiber and granola in it. Let's see what you brought us."

We walked back in together, and I offered him the treats. He went straight for a chocolate cake donut glazed in chocolate icing, and I could see from the donut that Emma had done me one better. She'd added chocolate chips to the mix as well. I'd have to taste one myself later. If it was anything as good as it looked, I had a feeling that I'd be adding her variation to our menu soon.

Bobby took a bite and smiled. "That's what I'm talking about. Man, that's good."

"I'll pass your compliments on to the chef," I said.

"You mean you didn't make these yourself?" he asked, clearly puzzled. "Don't tell me you buy them from a factory."

"Never," I said. "My assistant happened to make this batch."

"I get it. Why work when you've got someone else who can do it for you," he said.

That wasn't what I'd meant at all, but I wasn't going to push it. "I was speaking with your father earlier about who might have killed your great-grandfather."

"Let me guess. He tried to say it was Aunt Phyllis, didn't he?"

"As a matter of fact, he did," I said. "How did you know?"

"Those two have been natural enemies practically since birth, or so I've been told," he said as he demolished the chocolate donut and went after a Boston cream–filled one next.

"So, if she's not at the top of your list, then who is?"

"Perry Kilroy," he said firmly. "You should have heard the stories Jasper told me about that man. They weren't fit as bedtime tales, I can tell you that. It's a wonder he ever invited him here in the first place, and I think Perry realized he'd never get another shot at Jasper, so he seized the opportunity when he had it."

"But your great-grandfather invited him here to make amends, didn't he?"

Bobby shrugged. "That was the party line, but I wasn't buying it for a second. You should have seen the way Perry looked at him when he didn't think anyone was watching. It kind of made my blood run cold."

"Did you know about the hidden key?" I asked him. I'd meant to ask Ethan that same question, but we'd run out of time before he was going to throw us out. The only person I knew for a fact who knew was Phyllis, since she'd been the one to retrieve it the day before.

"As a matter of fact, the entire family knew about it," he said.

"But would Perry Kilroy know?" I asked as innocently as I could manage. Whoever had killed Jasper had to have known about the key, since Jake had told me the night before about needing a key to lock it from the inside or the outside, which was the way we'd found it when we'd first arrived on the scene.

"No, I didn't think about that," he said. "You know what? Maybe I'm wrong."

"It's hard to say at this point, isn't it?" I asked, trying to sound as sympathetic as I could manage, given the fact that this man might just have been the one who'd murdered my friend. "What about Henry?"

"What about him?" Bobby asked, barely slowing down as he finished the Boston cream and went in for a plain glazed donut as his next treat. If he kept that up, there wouldn't be any donuts left for anyone else.

"What's his story? At first I thought he was as meek as a mouse, but then he warned me to back away from Phyllis, and there was nothing meek about him then," I said.

"Yeah, I think he's got a spine in there somewhere, but he's afraid to offend my aunt in the slightest. I heard them arguing last night. It was about money, naturally enough, and I had to wonder if the man was stone-cold broke himself. If Phyllis doesn't get her inheritance, they both just might end up out on the street."

"Could Henry have killed Jasper so that Phyllis could get her inheritance?" I asked. If I hadn't seen that flare-up of his temper, I never would have believed it, but during those few moments, I'd realized that he might be capable of murder, for self-preservation if nothing else.

"I guess it's possible," Bobby said. He took one bite of the glazed donut, and then he threw it back in the box with the other pristine donuts. It was all I could do not to slap him, the act was one of such disregard for my offerings. "Thanks for the goodies," he said as he wiped his hands on his shirt, and then he walked out.

I grabbed a napkin, wrapped it around his discarded donut,

and then I threw it away. If he came looking for it later, which I hoped he did, maybe he'd realize the rudeness of his act.

I was about to head out to look for Phyllis and Henry when the door opened again. I'd been dreading the fact that Ethan was coming back soon, so it surprised me to see that Bethesda Long was there instead.

"Bethesda, what are you doing here? I thought the party was your sole obligation to the Finneys," I said.

"I could ask you the same thing, but as I told you before, my family and the Finneys have known each other for decades. When my father died on the job, Jasper stepped in and helped my family through some tough times. That explains my presence, but I repeat, why are you here?" she asked haltingly. It was obvious that she'd been just as surprised to discover me in the kitchen as I'd been finding her there.

"I delivered fresh donuts for breakfast this morning," I said, glad yet again that I'd been creative enough to bring a dozen treats with us. It never ceased to amaze me how good they were at getting me into places I could not otherwise visit.

"I'm sure they would have had plenty to eat without your donation," she said as she surveyed the kitchen's chaotic collection of food.

"Maybe, but they wouldn't have had as much fun eating them as they have," I said. Bethesda looked around as we talked, and I had to wonder if she'd lost something the day before. "Are you looking for something in particular?" I asked her.

"No, nothing of importance," she said. After glancing around the kitchen, she said, "It's clear there's nothing I can do here. I'm leaving."

"Thanks for coming by," I said with as straight a face as I could manage.

"Sure," she said, uncertain of exactly how to react to that. "I suppose I'll see you at the viewing tonight, or the funeral tomorrow."

"Are you going, too?" I asked her. "I'll be there, since I've known Jasper for years, but it surprises me that you'll be there."

"I thought it would be fitting for me to attend, given our history," she said.

I was about to reply when the kitchen door opened yet again. This place was getting busier than the beach at spring break.

At least this was the visit that I'd been expecting.

Ethan didn't look at all pleased to find me there with Bethesda. Phillip shrugged when no one else was looking in his direction. He'd given me more time than I'd had any right to expect, but it appeared that the opportunity was now over.

At least that's what I thought until I heard the doorbell ring.

With any luck, it would be yet another distraction for Ethan, and Phillip and I would have more opportunities to snoop around the place while we could.

CHAPTER 14

"SUZANNE. CHIEF. WHAT ARE YOU two doing here?" Chief Grant asked us the moment he saw us standing behind Ethan and Bethesda.

"We brought donuts," I said lamely.

It didn't impress him nearly as much as I'd hoped it would. "Uh huh. I need to see Perry Kilroy," he told Ethan officiously.

"I haven't seen him all morning," Ethan said, and then he turned to Bethesda. "Have you?"

"I just got here myself," she said. "I have no idea where the man is."

"Why is that, by the way? Why are you here?" Ethan asked her. "You understand that we're under no obligation to pay you past yesterday, don't you?"

"This visit is free of charge. I'm doing it as a friend of the family," she said. "I just wanted to see if I could help out."

"I don't see how you could, but thanks for offering," he said coldly. "I do believe that you've done enough."

"I'll just be going then," she said as she walked past Chief Grant. "Excuse me."

"It's fine," the chief said, and then he turned back to Ethan. As long as he was ignoring us for the moment, that was all that I cared about. "Where is Mr. Kilroy staying?"

"Somewhere upstairs," Ethan said as he waved his hand in that general direction. "You'll have to go look for yourself."

"Why don't you show me?" the chief asked. It was clear that it was not a request.

"Fine," Ethan said with a sigh. "Follow me."

As Jasper's grandson started up the stairs, the chief looked at me as I trailed behind him. "Seriously? You're going to push your luck with me even more?"

"We're just as curious about him as you are, Chief," Phillip said.

"You should know better, sir," Chief Grant told his former boss.

"I do, but I just can't seem to find enough caring inside for it to matter anymore," my stepfather said without a hint of regret or remorse in his voice.

"Coming, Constable?" Ethan asked as he paused at the top of the steps.

"It's Chief," the three of us corrected him simultaneously.

"Whatever. Perry Kilroy was given this room last night. If you'd care to wake him, be my guest. It's high time he was up, anyway."

The chief stepped up to the door and rapped on it soundly.

When there was no response, he tried it again.

"You don't suppose he's dead too, do you?" Ethan asked, clearly aghast at the prospect.

"There's only one way to find out," Chief Grant said as he pulled out his revolver and put his free hand on the doorknob. "I'm coming in," he announced loudly. With that, he opened the door and quickly stepped into the room.

It turned out that there had been no need for such dramatics.

The place was empty.

Not only that, but it was pretty obvious that the bed hadn't been slept in the night before, either.

It looked as though we had ourselves a runner.

"I don't understand this," Ethan said as he looked around the clearly empty room. "You told him to stay here last night, didn't you?"

"I did," Chief Grant said as he grabbed his radio. After reporting the man missing and putting out an alert for him, he turned back to us. "Don't worry. We'll find him soon enough."

"If you say so," Ethan said. "Now, if you'll excuse me, I have arrangements to see to in town."

"I won't keep you from it," Chief Grant said.

Ethan didn't even look in our direction as he left.

"Now, what am I going to do with the two of you?" the police chief asked once we were all alone.

"It's all really perfectly innocent," Phillip said, and he was beginning to explain when the current police chief shut him down.

"Save it, sir," he said, adding the last bit to make it a little easier to go down. "I'd appreciate it if you two would quit mucking about in my crime scene."

"Getting ready to solve it, are you?" Phillip asked him with a taunt in his voice.

"I'm following up on some solid leads and making real progress," Chief Grant said.

Phillip was clearly unimpressed. "Save it for Ray Blake. You can't doublespeak me, young man. You should know better."

"As a matter of fact, I do," Chief Grant said with a sigh. As he stood there, I could almost see the years being added to his face and posture. The job was wearing on him, and I wished that I could somehow help, but if there was any way for me to do it, I couldn't fathom what it might be. "Are you two about finished here?"

"If you don't mind, I'd love to speak with Phyllis and Henry, as long as we're here," I said, knowing that I should probably just shut up and count my blessings. Unfortunately, that had never been my strong suit.

"Well, you can't. They're in town at the moment making arrangements for Jasper's cremation and urn," he explained.

"How did you happen to know that?" I asked him.

"You two aren't the only ones trying to solve this case," Chief Grant said with another, longer sigh.

"For the record, I just came along to keep Suzanne company," Phillip said.

"Am I really supposed to believe that?"

"It's your choice, but you should know that it has the added benefit of being the total, unvarnished truth." Phillip's tone lightened considerably as he put a hand on his former officer's shoulder. "It's a stumper, Stephen. Don't beat yourself up about not solving it right away. Give yourself a break."

"Would you have?" the current chief asked.

"Of course not," Phillip said. "But then again, that's why I'm not on the job anymore. We'll get out of your hair. How does that sound?"

"I'd appreciate it," he said.

Once we were downstairs again, I asked Phillip, "What was that all about?"

"He needed a few words of encouragement. That's all," my stepfather explained.

"I'm not talking about that. Why did you volunteer for us to leave?"

"Who else was there for us to speak with? I was with you when you interviewed Ethan, and we overheard you chatting with Bobby on our way back. If you didn't grill Bethesda when you had the chance, then I must not know you very well after all."

"I spoke with her," I admitted. "She acted as though she was looking for something the entire time we were talking."

"Did she find it?" Phillip asked.

"If she did, I didn't notice what it possibly could have been. She gave up awfully quickly when Ethan suggested that she leave."

"What choice did she have?" he asked me. "It was practically an engraved invitation for her to get out, and not everyone is as brazen as you."

As we got into the Jeep to head back into town, I said, "Thanks for the diversion, by the way."

"I don't know what you're talking about," Phillip said with a grin.

"Okay, is that the way we're playing it?"

"I just want a clear conscience when I speak with your mother again," he admitted.

"Do you mean about the donuts?" I asked him with a smile.

"Hey, I thought we had an understanding about those," he said with a frown.

"We do. If she finds out, it won't be from me."

My stepfather took his phone out and started to dial.

"Who are you calling?"

"Your mother," he said.

"Don't give yourself up without a fight," I encouraged him.

"This call isn't about that. Hang on. Hey, Dot. Yes, Suzanne and I are having ourselves a little field trip. Of course we were at the Finney place. Hang on. Would you take a breath and let me get a word in edgewise?"

It was a daring tack to take with my mother, but I could hear her laughter on the other end of the phone. Phillip continued, "How hard would it be to find out about Jasper's will?"

I was about to protest that we already knew about it when he held up one hand to silence me. Wow, this man really was bold.

"No, not the current one. I want to know what the one before it said and when it was changed to the final version. Can you find that out without breaking too many laws or calling in too many favors? Yes, it might help Suzanne. Okay. We'll see you soon." After he hung up, he said, "She's on it."

"You want to know if the will was changed. I get that. It could give one of our suspects a motive if anything drastic changed. But why do you want to know *when* it happened? Hang on. Don't answer that. You want to know if everyone involved learned of the changes made *before* Jasper was murdered. Not bad, Chief."

"It's just Phillip these days," he said, though it was clear that he was pleased with the title, even if it had been given only temporarily. "Your mother is better at uncovering those things than I ever could be. Unless I miss my guess, she'll have the answers for us by the time we get there, unless you want to chase Phyllis and Henry down first. Hang on, that gives me another idea." Before I could say anything, he took his phone out again and dialed a new number. After asking a few questions, he ended the call. "They just left the mortuary, and they are on their way to Union Square for lunch. Unless you want to try to track them down there, I suggest we go see what your mother was able to find out."

"Sometimes I forget how good you could be at your job," I told him with a hint of admiration in my voice.

"What can I say? I had my moments," the former chief said.

When we got to the cottage that Phillip shared with my mother, I was surprised to find Momma standing out by the curb waiting for us. After I stopped, she hopped in the back.

"Were we going somewhere?" I asked her.

"Lunch," she said agreeably. "I'm starving."

My stomach began to grumble as well. We could go to Union Square and try to track down the last two folks I wanted to talk to, which might take hours, or we could go grab a bite at the Boxcar Grill, which also would give me the opportunity to check up on Trish. "How's the Boxcar Grill sound to you?" I asked.

"Where else?" Momma replied.

When we got there, the place was relatively empty, which was good for my chances of having a conversation with Trish but bad for business.

The owner seemed unusually chipper when we walked in.

"Did you find something out?" I asked her excitedly. "Is the ticket yours?"

"No, I'm afraid not," Trish said with a smile.

I was more than a little puzzled by her behavior. "Then why are you so happy?"

"Suzanne, I never realized it before, but until I found out that I *hadn't* won, I didn't quite get just how happy I was with my life the way it was right now," she explained.

"Did you at least *speak* with Logan?" Momma asked her.

"Oh, yes. He's good. In fact, it took him less than ten seconds to prove that I didn't have a claim on the money."

"I knew that he was able, but I never suspected he was capable of working miracles," Momma said. "How did he manage that?"

"He did something I failed to do. I'd made a copy of the front of the ticket as a precaution and put the real thing in my safe. He wanted to see the original, and that was that."

"Would someone please explain it to me?" I asked them.

"The ticket was already endorsed in someone else's name," Momma guessed.

"You are correct. The real winner has promised me a finder's fee, but I doubt it will be enough to change my life," Trish said. "And you know what? That's just fine with me. Sit wherever you'd like."

"How are the girls in back taking it?" I asked, wanting to know their moods before I placed my order.

"They couldn't be any happier," she said. "All is right with my world again."

"Happy to hear it," I said, and then I hugged her. "As long as you're pleased with the outcome, then so am I."

"Hey, don't get me wrong. It was fun being rich for a little bit, but honestly, it caused me more headaches than I ever could have imagined," Trish said.

After we placed our orders, I marveled as the grill owner seemed to skip as she walked away. "I never would have figured that for an outcome," I said.

"It doesn't surprise me a bit," Momma said. "Life can be a real burden when it comes to having money."

"Fortunately, that's something I don't have to worry about running Donut Hearts," I said with a smile.

"Someday you will, though," Momma said. If she was implying that she wasn't going to be with me forever, I didn't want to hear it. I couldn't imagine my life without my mother in it. In fact, the mere thought of it would send me into a spiraling depression that I might never recover from, so I did the adult thing.

I chose to stick my head in the sand and ignore that it would ever be a possibility.

"Did you have any luck getting the info about Jasper's will Phillip asked you about?" I asked her, pretending to study my surroundings, though I knew them almost as well as I knew my donut shop.

"I was able to speak with someone at the courthouse who was most helpful," she said. "The will was changed only four days ago."

"Wow, that was quick," I said. "Who was added? Bobby?"

"No, as a matter of fact, it was Ethan's name that had been absent until then."

That was a real shocker. "So, Bobby and Phyllis were going to split everything, and Jasper was cutting his own grandson out of the picture entirely?"

"That sums it up," Momma said. "I took the liberty of making a few other calls, and it turns out that Ethan has been written into and out of Jasper's will at least half a dozen times over the past three years. They would reconcile, then they would fight, and then they would reconcile again."

I frowned. "I don't like the sound of that."

"Some families are just that way, Suzanne," Momma said.

"That's not what I meant. If Ethan wasn't sure how long he'd be in the will this time, it might give him enough incentive to make sure that this version was Jasper's truly last will and testament."

"I hadn't thought of it that way," Momma said.

Phillip patted my hand. "Good work, Detective," he said.

"I'm no detective," I said as I felt a blush begin.

"I beg to differ. Wow, that was quick." Phillip was commenting on the arrival of three specials. The plates were heaped with meatloaf smothered in sauce, green beans that looked fresh, not canned, and loaded mashed potatoes that contained several secret additions of their own.

"Three specials," Trish said as she delivered them with a flourish.

As the three of us ate, we talked about a great many things, but my mind kept going back to Ethan Finney. Could he have slain his own grandfather just to get out of debt? I knew the answer to that without even having to voice it as a question to the others. Over the years, I'd seen people commit a variety of vile acts in the name of greed. Then again, just because Ethan had been included in the latest version of Jasper's will didn't mean that Bobby or Phyllis were necessarily innocent. Evidently they all had a desperate need for money. That left Perry Kilroy on my list, whose missing status didn't help me believe that he was innocent of the murder. Bethesda Long seemed to keep popping up as well, but I didn't have a motive for her.

At least not yet.

"Momma, how good are your ties in Union Square?"

"They are fairly strong," she replied as she took another bite of meatloaf. "Is that green pepper I'm tasting? Yes, I'm sure of it. There's something else, though. Barbeque sauce, perhaps?"

"You can get the recipe later," I said, not meaning to snap at my mother but barking at her a little nonetheless. Phillip gave me a look that said I'd overstepped my boundaries, not that I'd needed it. "I'm sorry, Momma. I'd just like to know about Bethesda Long and how she might be a part of what's been happening at the Finney estate besides planning Jasper's party."

"Is there something you haven't shared with me about her?" Phillip asked me.

"No. I just can't help wondering what she was looking for this morning," I admitted. "Besides, she seemed to be everywhere yesterday, and no one notices a party planner if they show up in unexpected places, do they? It would be the perfect cover to move around without anyone realizing that they were doing more than planning an event, wouldn't it?"

"You have a suspicious mind," Phillip said.

"Watch it, dear. That's my daughter you're talking about," Momma warned him.

"It was a compliment, I assure you," Phillip replied.

"That's certainly how I took it," I said quickly, rushing to his defense.

My mother seemed bemused by us taking up for each other, so she let it drop. "Let me ask around. How much time do I have?"

"At least until dessert," I said, laughing.

"I may need more than that," Momma replied. "For the moment, all I want to do is enjoy this wonderful meal."

"I second it," Phillip said quickly.

"And I'll third it," I chimed in.

After we finished eating, Phillip asked me, "So, what's on tap for this afternoon? I'd be happy to go with you if you have more sleuthing scheduled."

"I'd love to, but Emma and I have to make another batch of donuts this afternoon," I said.

"Whatever for? Is there another party?" Momma asked.

"I wouldn't call it that, but some folks might. Jasper paid me in advance to make a batch of donuts for his wake," I admitted.

"I didn't realize you'd have to get started so soon," Phillip said.

"You knew about this?" Momma asked him.

"Hey, Suzanne and I are like this," he said as he displayed two crossed fingers.

"He saw me reading the letter today I got from Jasper before he died," I admitted. I reached for the check, but Momma was quicker. "I was going to pick that up," I protested.

"You may get it the next time," Momma said.

"You always say that, but you never let me do it," I said.

"Consider it a mother's prerogative. Now you be careful, do you hear me?"

"Making donuts? What kind of trouble can I get into doing that?" I asked.

"I don't know, but you often manage to find a way," she replied.

I grinned at her before I answered. "I'd argue with you about that, but it happens to be true." Once we were outside, I surprised both Momma and Phillip by giving her a hug and then him. "Thanks for going with me this morning."

"Any time," he said with a smile.

"I'll be glad to drop you both off before I go to work," I volunteered.

"I believe the walk will do us good, given what we just consumed," Momma said. "Keep us posted," she said, and Phillip just waved as they headed off for home on foot.

I was crossing the street to go to Donut Hearts when I realized that someone was out front waiting for me.

Two someones, as a matter of fact.

CHAPTER 15

"I'M SURPRISED TO SEE YOU both here. I heard you were in Union Square," I told Phyllis and Henry as I reached for my keys. I didn't think they'd try anything in broad daylight, but then again, what did I know? Was it worth risking my life over, just in case I was wrong?

"We were, but we came back to see you instead. Suzanne, frankly, we're worried," Phyllis said, showing me a vulnerable side I hadn't seen before. "Henry convinced me that we should talk to you about Jasper's death before something else happened."

"Murder, you mean," I said as I put my key in the lock. The more I thought about it, though, I was probably safer outside with them than I'd be in the donut shop. At least out where we were, people driving by, visiting the Boxcar Grill, ReNEWed, or The Last Page, might see us.

"You're right. Murder," she said as she looked around. "Must we talk out here? I feel so exposed."

"I'd rather, if you don't mind," I said.

"She doesn't trust us," Henry said calmly. "And really, can you blame her?" Gone was the dangerous version of the man I'd witnessed before, but I knew that he might not be very far away.

"No, I suppose not," she said. "Very well. May we at least sit down? It's been a trying day, and it's only going to get worse."

"We can do that," I said as I moved over to one of the chairs we kept outside for our customers. It was also where Emma and I took our breaks mid-donut run, though that normally happened during what most folks thought of as the middle of the night.

After we were all settled in, Henry prompted his companion. "Go on, Phyllis. Tell her."

"First of all, I want to say that I didn't kill my grandfather, and neither did Henry."

"I wish that was all that it took," I said, "but nobody's going to believe either one of you without some sort of proof to back it up."

"Would it help if we didn't have motives?" Henry asked.

"It might," I replied.

Henry sighed, and then he nodded once. "I don't like to mention this, but the fact is, Phyllis doesn't need the money from the inheritance, and I certainly don't either."

"Why is that? I was under the impression that you were both just scraping by," I replied, watching them closely.

"Far from it, as a matter of fact," Phyllis said. "Just because we live beneath our means doesn't mean that we're broke. Not at all."

"Where did this supposed money come from all of a sudden?" I asked. It was probably a rude question, but in a way, that was kind of what I did, ask things that others were afraid to.

"It's not all of a sudden at all. Have you heard the song from the seventies called, "Truly, Truly, Truly Yours"?"

"Of course I have," I said. "It's been on the radio forever, and I've heard it in at least a dozen movies over the years."

"Don't forget the commercials," Phyllis said.

"My dad wrote it," Henry said softly.

"Your father was Dylan McDylan?" I asked incredulously. Dylan was a pop star who had enjoyed a twenty-year solo career, and then, at the height of his fame, he'd died suddenly in a car crash, leaving behind a wife and small baby. "You're Little Henry," I said. "Just like in the song."

"Yes, just like in the song," Henry admitted. "Mom passed away five years after Dad died. They said it was due to complications from surgery, but I knew it was from a broken heart. She never got over my father's death. The thing is, I was her only heir."

"And all of the rights passed on to you?"

Henry nodded. "Dad was a stickler for owning the copyright on every song he ever wrote. No matter who covered it or how it was used, he got paid for it. He was a pretty savvy businessman as well as a performer."

"If anything, Henry has even grown the brand more since he took over the estate," Phyllis said proudly. "But not for his personal gain. He runs a charitable foundation that does a great deal of good, but that doesn't mean that we're not comfortable beyond my wildest expectations."

"Okay, money might not have been a motive for you, but how about something else? Convince me that you didn't kill him," I said.

"Jasper and I were reconciling," Phyllis said. "I know how I come off when I'm around my family. I revert to some kind of shrew. They know every button to push, and they seem to delight in pressing them. Ethan does, at any rate. Jasper and I were working things out, though. He was even going to give me away at my wedding," she said. "Ask Bobby. He knows all about it."

"Not Ethan?" I asked her.

"My brother was always the black sheep of the family," she admitted. "No one but a few folks know that he was in and out of my grandfather's will like a revolving door. My guess is that he jumped on the opportunity to kill him while he was currently in Jasper's good graces."

It gave me chills realizing that Phyllis's scenario was much like one of my own. "What about Bobby?"

"He means well. Frankly, he's a little impulsive, but considering who raised him, he's a model citizen."

"You don't have any real love for your brother, do you?" I asked her.

"If he'd been found dead, I would have probably turned myself in, whether I'd done it or not. Goodness knows there's enough history between us to lead the police to the conclusion that I did it. But not Jasper. Never Jasper."

Phyllis looked truly upset about her grandfather's death. This was a different woman than I'd seen so far. Was she acting, or was this the real Phyllis Carlisle? That was the question. I didn't think Henry was lying, though. His story would be too easy to check, not that I was going to take it at face value. After all, the one thing most liars were really good at was lying.

"You knew about the key to the study, though," I said, trying to answer every question I had about the pair.

"So did Ethan, and Bobby too, as a matter of fact," she said. "For all I know, Bethesda knew about it as well. She spent a great deal of time with Jasper planning his party over the past few months, and they got close."

"How close?" I asked her.

"It's not what you're thinking. There wasn't anything romantic between them. At least I don't think there was," she added doubtfully.

"Couldn't Perry Kilroy know about the key, too?" I asked.

"He didn't, though," Phyllis reminded me. "I may not care for the man, but he seemed genuinely surprised that the door was even locked."

"At least he acted that way," Henry said.

Phyllis frowned for a moment before she answered. "Somebody should probably talk to him."

"The police tried, but Perry Kilroy ran," I said.

"He took off?" Phyllis asked. "Doesn't that just scream that he's guilty?"

"I don't know. Maybe he just felt like getting away," I offered.

"Are you on his side, Suzanne?" Henry asked me coolly.

"There's one thing you should have no doubt in your mind about. I'm not on anyone's side but Jasper's," I said.

"Well, so are we," Phyllis said. "I just wanted you to know that Henry and I weren't involved with what happened."

"You don't happen to have alibis to seal the deal, do you?" I asked.

"Only each other," Henry said with the first hint of a wry grin I'd seen him sport. He knew as well as I did how worthless their corroboration was. "The thing is, Phyllis hates being considered a suspect in her own grandfather's murder. Can you blame her?"

"Of course not," I said. I saw Emma approaching, but she hesitated when she noticed that I was talking with a pair of strangers. She lifted both eyebrows in the form of a question, and I nodded in reply. As she approached, I stood. "I appreciate you both coming down to the donut shop, but if I'm going to make treats for your grandfather's wake, I'd better get started."

"I didn't know that was even happening," Phyllis said. "Surely Ethan didn't order them."

"As a matter of fact, Jasper did," I said.

"What? How is that even possible?"

"He made the request the day before he died. In fact, he even paid in advance," I explained.

"He must have had a feeling that something was going to happen to him," Henry said sagely.

"That's the growing consensus. Now, if you'll excuse me, I need to get busy."

"Of course," Henry said as he took Phyllis's arm gently.

"What was that all about?" Emma asked me as she joined me at the door to Donut Hearts.

"Honestly? I'm not completely sure," I answered. "Sorry to drag you back in after you worked all morning here twice in two days."

"That's okay," she said. "I'm happy to help out."

"I know, but you're not doing it for free," I replied as I pulled Jasper's hundred out of my pocket and handed it to her.

"What's this?" she asked me.

"It's what Jasper gave me to make donuts for his wake," I explained. "I want you to have all of it."

"What about your expenses? You should at least recoup those," Emma said, refusing the money.

"No, this one's on me. It's my way of honoring an old friend."

Emma frowned. "Why can't I honor him, too? Put that to good use somewhere else. I'm working for free today, too."

"Emma, you don't have to do that," I said, trying to push the bill on her yet again.

"I know I don't. I want to, though." She frowned, and then it suddenly blossomed into a full-tilt grin. "I've got an idea."

"I'm listening," I said.

"Let's donate it to the soup kitchen in Jasper's name. I know they'd be delighted to get it, and think about how many people we can feed in his memory."

I put the bill on the counter and hugged my assistant. "Emma Blake, you are an amazing young woman. You know that, don't you?"

Emma said lightly in my ear, "That's what I keep telling everybody, but no one seems to want to listen."

I pulled my head back so I could look her straight in the eye. "I'm serious."

"So am I," she said as she pulled away with a smile. "Why don't you take the lead this afternoon? After all, you probably miss working in the donut shop; it's been so long since you were here last."

I laughed. "I know you're teasing, but in a way, it's true. This place has a way of getting into your blood."

"You don't have to tell me," she said. "Now, what can I do, boss?"

"Start folding boxes while I get the cake donut batter ready," I said with a smile.

"You've got it."

It was going to be a small run, all cake donuts and no yeast ones, so today was going to go much faster than the day before had. That was a good thing. I wanted to get the order knocked out, go home and take a quick shower and change, and then deliver them to the Finney estate in time for the wake. I wouldn't mind if Jake—or even Grace—got back in time to help, but if neither one of them did, I'd be fine making my delivery on my own.

"By the way, I saw the paper this morning," I told Emma as I finished glazing the last of the cake donuts. All that was left on my end was to ice a handful of others with a chocolate glaze, and the donuts needed to cool a little before I did that. My assistant was in hot, soapy water up to her elbows, and she couldn't have seemed any happier. I was fortunate to have her, both in my business and my life, and I made sure that a day didn't go by that I didn't tell her that.

"What did you think?" she asked me neutrally.

"I have to say that your dad did a fair job," I admitted.

"I especially liked the pictures you took," she said with a grin. "They were hilarious."

The front page had featured a shot Ray had to have taken himself of the front of the house. He'd manipulated the image to make it dark and oppressive. I knew that most legitimate newspapers frowned on photo manipulation of any kind, but Ray was a law in and of himself. His paper had more of a feel of a tabloid than a real newspaper, though I would never dream of saying anything like that to the editor's face. He prided himself on the *April Springs Sentinel*, and woe to the person who denigrated it in front of him. Inside the paper, where it mattered much less, were some of the photos that Jake had taken. Try as he might, even Ray and his liberal use of artistic license couldn't make those images very interesting.

"I have a gift for photography, wouldn't you say?"

"Some people might," Emma said with a laugh. "I don't mean me, but some people. Did you read the story?"

"I did," I admitted. "On the whole, it wasn't as overly dramatic as I worried it might be."

"How did you like all of the attributes to 'two unnamed sources on the scene'? I take it Jake was informant number two?"

"I couldn't say," I said with a full-blown grin. "I'm still trying to figure out who the first source of information was."

"I wonder," Emma said with a giggle.

After I let Emma out, I surveyed the boxes of donuts on hand, ready for delivery. I was proud of her, of us, actually, for contributing the money Jasper had paid me to the soup kitchen. This was indeed our tribute to the man we'd lost: a customer and a friend.

But I couldn't deliver them smelling like a donut shop, no matter how enticing my husband found the aroma. I had time, if I hurried, to go home, take a quick shower, change clothes, and still make my delivery before the wake began.

I locked up the shop and headed home, hoping to see Jake's truck or even Grace's company car on the short drive there.

Unfortunately, neither one of those things happened.

I grabbed a quick shower, shampooing my hair carefully to get the last remnants of donut smell out. I was never entirely successful at it, but I could take care of most of it, at any rate. After getting dressed, I started toweling off my hair, trying to dry it as naturally as I could. I wasn't a big fan of blow dryers, especially in the warmer months.

As I worked on my hair, I stood idly in front of my computer and reviewed the images Jake and I had downloaded into it after we'd found the body. It was tough seeing Jasper like that, and I tended to stay on those images much less than I did on the surrounding shots. I smiled as I spotted the photos Jake had taken with Ray's camera. Try as he might, the newspaper editor hadn't been able to glam up those pictures, no matter what he'd tried. Flipping back to the shots I'd taken, I focused on the desktop in front of Jasper. There were scattered pens and mechanical pencils all over the blotter. Their holder had been tipped over, no doubt in the final throes of Jasper's dying breath. Was that where the letter opener had been? How had the killer managed to take it without Jasper realizing it? Had they casually leaned over and taken it, pretending to study it all the while preparing to commit murder, or had it been a violent grab before the killer had plunged it into Jasper's heart from behind? Next, I studied the shot of Jasper's chair and the hard plastic mat that it rolled across. There were several scuff marks, but who knew how long they'd been there? I started going through photo after photo of the crime scene, trying to make some sense of it all. Images of the office itself, the exterior, even the hallway flitted across my field of vision as I jumped from frame to frame to frame.

I was still studying the images, wondering if there was something I was missing that I just couldn't place my finger on, when my cell phone rang.

"Hey, stranger. I was hoping you'd be back home by now," I said the moment I knew that it was Jake.

"Unfortunately, it's taking a little longer than I'd hoped. How are things going there?"

"Phyllis and Henry might be out as suspects," I said as I explained their story. "What do you think?"

"If it's true, then the money doesn't really matter, and that seems to be the driving force, at least as far as we've been able to determine so far," he said.

"Hang on a second. Let me check something." I closed out the pictures and opened up a search engine on the Internet. After typing in the relevant data, I found a few images of Henry, as well as substantiation that he was, in fact, rich and also that he ran a charitable foundation.

"If I'm keeping you from something, I could always call you back later," Jake said with a laugh in his voice.

"I just confirmed that Henry's story is true," I said.

"The marvels of the Internet age," Jake said with a sigh. "It's going to make detectives obsolete some day."

"You don't believe that for one second, and you know it," I said.

"Of course I don't, but you'd be amazed by the number of people who do. Sorry. I'm just a little stale from these meetings. It's going to be at least a few more hours before I can get away, and that's if I'm lucky."

"I feel for you," I said as I shut my computer down.

"What's on tap for you?"

"I'm just getting ready to deliver donuts to the wake, and then I'm free," I said.

"Is Grace going out there with you?" Jake asked me. "Or Phillip?"

"On a donut run? I'm pretty sure I can handle that on my own."

He paused, and then he said, "I'd still rather you didn't go by yourself."

I was about to answer when I saw that I was getting another call. "Hang on. That's Grace on the other line."

"Saved by the ring," he said. "I've got to go. Just be careful, okay?"

"You bet," I said, and then I switched over to Grace. "Hey, what's up?"

"I figured out what Minerva's problem was," she said. "It took most of the afternoon, but I finally got it out of her."

"Why did she want to quit?"

"Her trainer told her if she was ever caught using samples for her personal use, she'd be terminated immediately, as well as potentially being prosecuted for theft."

"Is that true? I seem to recall you carrying around a bag full with you most of the time," I reminded her.

"Of course it's not true. That's one of the perks of the job, as far as I'm concerned. I called Debbie to straighten it out, and she swore she said not to take cases of it for her own use but that individual samples were fine. Minerva was so relieved that she started crying, and I just got her settled down enough so I could leave. She thought we were going to have her arrested for using a little lipstick. Can you believe that?"

"I believe anything at this point," I said. "At least she's honest."

"Too honest for sales, maybe, but we'll see," Grace said. "Anyway, I'm an hour away from town, so if you're up for a little more investigation, I'm game."

"Sounds good to me," I said, purposefully neglecting to mention that I was making a donut delivery to the crime scene. I'd already gotten one lecture on being careful, and I wasn't in the mood for another. "Give me a buzz when you get home."

"You bet," Grace said, and then I hung up before she could ask me any more questions.

It was time to collect the donuts and make my promised delivery.

After that, I was going to focus all of my energy on finding Jasper's killer, no matter what it took.

It turned out, though, that was going to happen even sooner than I'd anticipated, or I might have taken Jake's advice and taken along a buddy with me after all.

CHAPTER 16

I WAS JUST LOADING THE DONUTS into my Jeep when I heard someone pulling up beside me. It was a squad car, and Chief Grant got out, grinning.

"What are you so happy about?" I asked him with a smile of my own.

"We got Perry Kilroy," he said. "I told you we would."

"Did he confess to killing Jasper?" I asked him. While Perry had been on my radar, I'd been primarily focused on the murder victim's family members, not his former business partner.

"No, but it's just going to be a matter of time, unless I miss my guess," the chief said. "Why else would he run if he didn't have something to hide?"

"Maybe he wasn't in the mood to be run through the wringer at his age," I offered.

"If that's the case, then he surely chose the wrong way to avoid it." The police chief's radio beeped, and he turned to me and said, "Hang on one second."

"Mind if I keep loading donuts?" I asked him.

He shrugged, which I took as agreement, and I got back to work.

After a minute of hushed conversation, he didn't look nearly as happy as he had when he'd first approached me.

"Did something else happen?"

"Kilroy has lawyered up," the chief said. "He's bringing in some kind of dream team, and they won't even let him admit to his own name. It figures. Having money can't buy freedom, but it can surely delay incarceration."

"So, do you really think he did it?"

The chief shrugged. "Nine times out of ten, fleeing is tantamount to confessing. Anyway, I saw you out here loading donuts and thought I'd check in with you." He surveyed my loaded Jeep before adding, "It's awfully late to be making a donut delivery, isn't it?"

"This is a special case," I said.

"Just like yesterday?" he asked me with a smile. "How special can it be if you do it every day?"

"Okay, that was a special case, too, but they really are rare. These are for Jasper's wake."

Chief Grant nodded. "I always knew that the man had style."

"He'll be missed," I agreed.

"No doubt. Well, I'd better get going. I've got a mound of paperwork to fill out before Grace gets back. We're going out to the Boxcar tonight to celebrate. Would you and Jake like to join us?"

"That depends," I said. "What are we celebrating?"

"Trish not winning the lottery," the chief said with a smile.

"That's kind of cruel, isn't it?" I asked him.

"Hey, it was Trish's idea, so blame her. What do you say?"

"Count us in," I replied.

"You aren't even going to check with Jake first?" he asked me lightly.

"I can't imagine that it will be too difficult talking him into eating at his favorite place in town with two of our best friends," I replied.

"Then it's a double date," the chief said.

I loved being a part of our tight-knit community. We celebrated our joys together and shared our woes as well. It just so happened that I was about to do both, in a rather short period of time. I appreciated the order of things, though. First the wake and then the celebration that Trish had gotten what she wanted in the end. It was only fitting that it had unfolded that way.

As I drove to the estate, something kept nagging at the back of my mind. I'd seen something in those photos that had set off a delayed alarm, but Jake's telephone call, as welcome as it had been, had thrown me off and made the idea slip away. Maybe it would come to me later, but in the meantime, I had a delivery to make.

Bobby answered the door, wearing jeans and a faded old T-shirt.

"Donut delivery!" I announced.

"Yeah, Dad told me you were coming. Is it just you?" he asked as he looked around behind me. It was a suspicious question, given what had been happening lately.

"Yes, but several people know that I'm here," I said. "Shall I bring them in?"

"I didn't mean that to sound so creepy," Bobby answered. He must have seen something in my expression that told him I was uneasy about his question. "I just meant that it's a lot to carry by yourself."

"I plan on making more than one trip," I said.

"Why don't I help you?" he volunteered.

"It's really not necessary," I told him as I shifted the weight of the boxes in my hands. It wasn't that they were particularly heavy, but four dozen donuts in boxes was an awkward thing to just stand around holding, and I had more in the Jeep.

"Come on. Let me help. It will give me something to do. I've been going stir-crazy sitting around listening to my dad and my aunt argue for the past two hours. Every now and then, Henry tries to get them to behave themselves, but I'm afraid that it's a lost cause."

"Is it just the four of you?" I asked as I handed the boxes in my hands to him so I could grab more.

"No, Bethesda's hovering around here someplace, too. She keeps telling Dad that she wants to honor Jasper's wishes, and he keeps asking her to leave. I've got to admit, it makes for a nice break from hearing him argue with my aunt."

As we took the first load into the living room where Bobby requested they be placed, I asked, "Are any other family or friends coming by?"

"Why do you ask?"

"It's just that we made a lot of donuts for four people," I said, "five if you count Bethesda."

"We're opening the place up later for other folks, but for the first hour, it's going to be just the three of us. Henry has even been asked politely to step away, and so has Bethesda. Why on earth my dad and my aunt want it to be just the three of us is beyond me."

"I heard about the will. It's sure to be a sizeable amount, even a third of it," I said, trying to gauge Bobby's reaction.

"Truthfully, the money will come in handy, but I'd rather have Jasper back," he said. "I'll probably just end up gambling my inheritance away, anyway."

It was a surprising moment of truth for him, and I could feel his vulnerability in that moment. That was the problem with some people. Just when I thought I had them pegged, they turned out to have a completely different side to them. I'd written Phyllis off as a money grubber, and it had turned out that she didn't need cash at all. I'd thought that Bobby was a flighty gambler with a poor sense of self-restraint, and that was probably at least partially right, but he also had clearly cared for his great-grandfather. "It doesn't have to be that way, you know."

"What do you mean? Are you talking about joining Gamblers Anonymous or something?"

"It couldn't hurt. You also might want to put what you get into a trust. That way you can set it up to get only ten percent a year."

"So then I'd blow it in ten years instead of one," he mused.

"I didn't mean it that way," I apologized.

"I didn't take it that way. I think it's the best idea I've heard all week. It may just give me time to get my act together before the money's all gone."

Ethan joined us, and the difference in attire between him and his son was remarkable. Instead of the casual look Bobby was currently sporting, his father was wearing a three-piece black suit with a crimson tie. His shoes had been polished to the point of nearly blinding me, and every hair on his head was in perfect place. "Hadn't you better start getting ready?" he asked his son.

Bobby nodded. "I guess. I still can't believe I have to wear a suit."

"Jasper left a contingency fund for all of us to be able to dress appropriately for his farewell," Ethan said. "It would be disrespectful to reject it."

So, that explained how the nearly bankrupt businessman could afford to dress so nicely. Was there anything that Jasper *hadn't* planned? He must have known deep in his heart that his days were truly numbered, and he'd acted accordingly. I myself wished he had just run away, leaving everyone behind and moving to some deserted island or mountaintop where his killer wouldn't have been able to get to him.

It would have been a far better use of his money, at least as far as I was concerned.

"I'm going," Bobby said. "I was just giving Suzanne a hand."

"Suzanne should have brought enough help with her to do her work," Ethan said primly.

"You're right. I should have," I said with a smile, though that wasn't my initial reaction. I didn't yet know if Ethan was culpable in Jasper's death, and if he wasn't, I knew that I needed to be cordial to one of Jasper's last living relatives.

"Is that all?" Ethan asked.

"No, I have a few more boxes I need to go get," I said.

"Then we won't keep you, will we, Bobby?" he asked his son pointedly.

"No, sir. Thanks, Suzanne."

"Hey, I'm the one who should be thanking you. You offered to help, and I'm grateful for it. Why are you thanking me?"

"First, the donuts smell delicious. If I have to eat another casserole, I'm not going to make it."

"And second?" I asked him.

"You broke the tension up around here, at least for a little bit."

Ethan grimaced at his son. "What tension is that, exactly?"

"Nothing, Dad. Forget I said anything," Bobby answered, and then he left us.

"If you'll excuse me, I have to see about some of our arrangements," Ethan said. "I trust you can handle the rest of your job by yourself."

"I'm not sure, but I'll surely give it my best shot," I said, letting a little of my sarcasm through after all. Oh, well. At least my intentions had been good initially.

"You should do that," Ethan said, and then he left the room to take care of whatever was so pressing. I couldn't imagine what it might be. It seemed to me that Jasper had already seen to everything needed for his final farewell.

I grabbed the last few boxes of donuts and carried them into the living room. I thought about arranging them on a platter like they'd been displayed before, so I headed off to the kitchen to see if I could find something to aid in my presentation. It was deserted, and I wondered where Bethesda was, since she and Henry had been told to make themselves scarce. As I started checking cupboards and cabinets for a suitable serving tray, something on the floor under one cabinet caught my eye.

Grabbing a tissue from my pocket, I bent over to retrieve it when I heard footsteps behind me.

Grabbing the object with the tissue and holding it tightly in my hand, I started to stand, pretending all the while that I hadn't just recovered something that might be of value to my investigation.

"What are you still doing here?" Ethan asked pointedly. "I thought you were leaving as soon as you finished with the delivery."

"I wanted to get a serving tray," I confessed. "My donuts look so much nicer when they're properly displayed."

"I'm sure we'll manage without the presentation," he said. Ethan practically grabbed my arm as he marched me to the front door.

I had wanted to try something to test my theory, but there was no way I was going to escape Jasper's grandson's notice this time. Ethan had made that mistake before, but evidently he had no intention of making it again.

"Again, I'm sorry for your loss," I said as he slammed the front door in my face.

It was as clear a signal as he could send, short of sic'ing the dogs on me, if they had dogs in the first place, which I knew for a fact that they didn't.

I wasn't ready to leave quite yet, though, even though technically, I was finished with my business there.

I had a few calls to make first to see if my hunch was right.

"Hey, Jake. Are you on your way home yet?"

"I am. I should be there in half an hour if I don't run into any traffic," he said when he answered his phone. "Where are you?"

"I just made my donut delivery to the Finney estate, and I'll have you know that I'm perfectly safe and sound."

"That's good news. Are you on your way back to the cottage?"

"Not exactly," I said. "As a matter of fact, I'm standing here leaning against the front of my Jeep chatting with you. I need you to call Chief Grant and ask him something for me. Could you do that?"

"Sure. What do you need to know?"

I told him, and to my husband's credit, he didn't ask any follow-up questions.

At least not yet.

"I'll get right back to you," Jake said.

"I'll be here," I replied.

"Suzanne, why don't you get in and start driving while I make this call? It won't matter in the end where you are when you get your answer, will it?"

"If it's all the same to you, I think I'll stay right where I am," I said.

"Okay. I know better than to waste my breath arguing with you. At least get in and sit in the front seat while you're waiting."

"Jake, the ragtop wouldn't stop a butter knife if someone were after me, and you know it," I protested. It was a beautiful day, and I didn't want to sit inside my vehicle if I didn't have to.

"Just indulge me, okay?" he asked.

"Fine, but I'm leaving my door open," I answered in protest as I did as he'd requested.

Jake hung up instead of answering, which was probably a favor to me. I knew I could vex my husband and try his patience at times, but I was equally sure that he wouldn't want me to be mousy and subservient, not that *that* was ever going to happen.

I heard back from him sooner than I had expected to. It only took him ninety seconds to get me an answer, and I had to wonder how long it would have taken me on my own.

"You were right," Jake said.

"So, Jasper didn't have a key on him when they searched the body, and the chief didn't find one there at the scene, either," I said.

"That's right," Jake said. "Suzanne, what's going on?"

"I was looking at some of the photos I took earlier on my phone, and there was one image taken facing the hallway that caught my eye," I admitted.

"What did you see? Are you talking about the garish carpet or the overcrowded furniture?"

"The carpet, or more precisely, what was on it," I said. "Something registered in my subconscious mind, but I didn't even realize what I was seeing until I added it to what I just found. Jake, I know who killed Jasper Finney!"

CHAPTER 17

"WELL, DON'T KEEP ME HANGING. Who did it, Suzanne?" Jake was nearly breathless waiting for my reply.

"The thing is that I know *who*, but I still don't know *why*," I said.

"We can figure out the motive once I know who you suspect. It's Ethan, isn't it?" he asked.

"I thought so too for the longest time, but no, it wasn't him."

"Who was it, then?" Jake asked, the impatience growing thick in his voice as he asked.

"Bethesda Long killed Jasper," I said.

"Bethesda? Why would she kill him?" Jake asked me. It was to his credit that he hadn't called me crazy, since I still hadn't told him my rationale.

"Let me back up. Do you remember that just after we found Jasper's body, Bethesda came into the hallway?"

"I wasn't there when it happened, but I remember you told me that you saw her," Jake said. "I was still inside with the body, remember?"

"That's right. Anyway, when she came to where I was standing, I told her the news, and she nearly fainted. In fact, she went so far as to put both hands on the floor to keep from toppling over, or so it seemed to me at the time."

"But that wasn't what she was doing, was it?" Jake asked, his voice now deadly serious.

"No, she was retrieving the only key to the study that she knew about. It was the one she took off Jasper's body after he was dead," I said. "I saw something shiny on the carpet in the photo, but I couldn't quite make it out. By the time Chief Grant's team got there, it was already gone. That's because Bethesda picked it up from where she first dropped it."

"Okay, but that's a little flimsy, isn't it?"

"Wait, there's more. The only thing I can figure out is that she must have had a hole in her pocket or something, because it fell out again in the kitchen. A little after the police arrived, I found her in there, obviously searching for something."

"How can you be sure it was the same key?" he asked me.

"Because I found it before she could. Right now, it's sitting in my pocket, safely wrapped in a tissue to protect the fingerprints."

"Suzanne, you need to get out of there right now," Jake ordered.

"You're right. I'm on my way. I'll talk to you soon," I said as I hung up and started to reach for my keys.

Unfortunately, I didn't get to them in time.

Bethesda Long quickly settled into the passenger seat after throwing open the door and climbing in beside me.

There was a long kitchen knife in her hand, and to make matters worse, it was pointed straight at my throat.

CHAPTER 18

"MY, MY, AREN'T YOU A clever girl," Bethesda said to me as she settled in.

"Not really. I don't know anything about anything," I replied, trying to keep my voice calm. I knew that one wrong move, and I was likely dead.

"You're too modest," the murderess said. "You were going to start the car and drive off. I suggest you do exactly that," she said.

"Listen, that was my husband on the phone. He'll be here in two minutes, Bethesda."

She took the blade and jabbed my sleeve with it, ripping the material and nicking my skin in the process.

"Oh!"

"Unless you want that to happen again, I suggest you get busy driving right now."

"Where are we going?" I asked her as I took my keys out and started the engine. The crazy woman didn't need to prod me more than once.

"I don't know. I feel like taking a drive, don't you?"

"What would you say if I gave you my keys and just got out of the Jeep?" I asked.

Bethesda jabbed me again, this time even harder than the last. The pain was sudden and intense, and as the blood ran down my arm, I protested, "If you don't quit stabbing me, I won't be able to drive."

"I'm sure you'll find a way somehow," she said. Her voice had taken on an eerie calm, and I had to wonder about her sanity.

It was certainly no time to challenge her, though.

I started to drive, wondering how I could leave Jake a sign that I had just been abducted by a stone-cold killer.

Nothing came to me, though, so I did as I was ordered.

For the moment, it was the only thing that I could do, the only thing that was keeping me alive.

I tried to make my driving seem random to her, but I was edging my way back toward April Springs, albeit via back roads. Hopefully, by the time she realized what I was doing, it would be too late. As an automatic gesture, I buckled my seatbelt, and then I glanced over at her. "You really should fasten your seatbelt, Bethesda."

"I believe if I'm apprehended, that will be the least of my worries," she said. "Make a right at the next stop sign."

"Are you sure you wouldn't rather go left?" I suggested, since that was the way back to town.

I was rewarded with another stab wound, this one to my leg.

"Hey!" I shouted. "Stop that!"

"Then stop disobeying me," she scolded me as though I were an errant pupil of hers.

I wasn't about to go against her wishes any more. I did as I was told, trying to think of something I could do that would hurt her and not me. The fact that she wasn't wearing a seatbelt could work in my favor if I played it right, but I needed a decent-sized tree in the right position before I tried to ram it. It was drastic, but that was what I was down to. Even if I perished in the crash as well, at least I'd go of my own volition, trying to free myself from my captor, not some kind of compliant victim just waiting to die.

Bethesda must have sensed what I was up to. The knife was now suddenly pressed against my neck, and I knew that one false move on my part would end in tragedy for me.

That managed to tame my rebellious streak rather quickly.

"Why did you kill him?" I asked as I continued to follow her random directions. She wasn't exactly making suggestions now. They were orders, and the next one I disobeyed might very well be my last. "I know *how* you did it, but I can't figure out why."

"It's simple enough. Jasper Finney killed my father."

"He *what*?" I asked, barely able to keep the Jeep's front tires on the narrow road. We were following a course I didn't recognize, I was hopelessly lost, and as the road grew tighter and tighter, my opportunity to successfully wreck us was fading fast.

"Oh, he didn't do it personally, but it was his equipment that killed my sweet old dad, so the blood was still on his hands. Dad didn't want to go to work that day. He knew what Jasper was making him do was too dangerous, but he had a family to support, and Jasper was insistent that it was safe. Only it wasn't."

"You said that Jasper took care of you and your family after your father died," I reminded her. "Surely that wasn't an act of a guilty man."

"To the contrary. He knew that he'd been responsible! The *only* reason he helped us was because he felt guilty."

"Did he know how you felt about him, even after all those years?" I asked. There was a tree ahead that might do if I could manage to accelerate enough into it to do some real damage. I hated hurting my precious Jeep, but I despised the prospect of dying even more.

"No, I hid it well, but when he invited me to plan his party, I knew that it was his way of telling me that he knew I held him culpable in my father's death. That's what this event was all about; making up for past wrongs. You see, I knew something that no one else knew, not even his family."

It was clear that she was dying to tell *someone* how clever she was. "What was that?"

"Jasper was dying. That's why he suddenly wanted to make amends all the way around. He didn't want to go to his grave with a guilty conscience about anything, but I robbed him of it. In the end, I won and he lost."

"How do you know he was dying?" I asked her, forgetting my plan for the moment.

"My mother had to go back to work after my father died," she said. "Guess where she still works to this day."

"The hospital," I said dully. It was all coming together, albeit a little too late to do me any good.

"Bingo. When she told me that he was dying, I knew that I had to act fast."

"I have a silly question. Why not just let him die of natural causes?" I asked as I got closer and closer to the tree. I tried to accelerate slightly so she wouldn't notice but still get up enough speed to hit it with some kind of impact.

"Then he would win!" she shouted. For a single instant, she let the knife drop, and I knew it was time to act.

One way or the other, this was going to be over, and soon.

CHAPTER 19

Fighting every instinct I had in my body, I jammed the accelerator down and jerked the wheel of my Jeep straight into the tall oak.

And for a moment, the world faded to black.

No matter what the outcome ended up being, it was out of my hands now.

CHAPTER 20

THANKFULLY, I WASN'T OUT LONG. When I came to, I could hear Bethesda moaning in the seat beside me. Without a seatbelt to restrain her from the impact, she'd been thrown partially into the windshield.

There was a great deal of blood on her face as well as her blouse, and I wondered how long she had to live.

I was in agony, both from the knife wounds and the wreck itself, but I somehow managed to undo my seatbelt and crawl out of the Jeep despite the pain. At least it was an older model without airbags. I wasn't sure how that might have changed things, but I hadn't had time to worry about it before I'd hit the tree.

Instead of calling Jake, I hit the emergency button on my phone.

It directed me straight to 9-1-1.

"There's been an accident," I said as a heavy fog seemed to cloud my mind.

"Suzanne? Is that you?"

"Yes, this is Suzanne, Suzanne Hart," I said, not knowing who was on the other end of the phone or even caring at that point. "I don't know where I am, but I was just in a car wreck."

"Describe your location to me," the disembodied voice on the other end of the line asked.

"Can't you just trace the call?" I asked. Why were they pushing me when all I wanted to do was drop down to the ground and rest? "There are trees, and a small path that's barely a road. Trace the call! Please!" I was on the verge of losing it, and I knew it.

"That will take too long. Come on, you can do it."

In a haze, I did the best I could to describe the twists and turns I'd taken, but I wasn't at all sure that I'd done a very good job of it.

If a twig behind me hadn't snapped at precisely the right moment, I would have been dead soon after.

But I wasn't.

At least not yet.

I looked up to see a bloody nightmare approaching me. Bethesda's face was wrecked, and so were her clothes. There was an amazing amount of blood on her, and yet she still managed to move toward me with crazy speed and a look of sheer determination on her face that I prayed I never saw again in my life, no matter how long that happened to be.

I did all I could do.

I threw my phone at her, and then I started to run away.

This woman wasn't human.

By all rights she should have died on impact, but she was clearly in better shape right now than I was.

As I ran away—stumbled, more like it—I could hear her behind me, getting closer and closer with every step I took.

My cut leg was aching, and so was my arm.

I'd also bruised my rib cage against the seatbelt in the wreck.

At the moment, my top speed wouldn't have beaten a lazy turtle.

I knew that if I stayed my course, I wasn't going to last much longer, so I did my best to change directions and start off into the woods.

Bethesda followed, but I could hear her slowing a little.

It wasn't much, but I'd take whatever I could get.

Was that the sound of road noise ahead of me? It could have just been the blood rushing in my ears, but then again, what did I have to lose? I headed toward it, somehow finding new energy in a final attempt to save my own life.

It was a road after all, and what was more, there were even a few cars on it.

I didn't even hesitate.

I jumped in front of the closest car, waving my hands frantically for the driver to stop.

He wasn't able to, though.

In an effort to avoid running me over, he jerked the steering wheel to the right, and I heard a sickening crumpling sound just behind me.

Evidently he'd missed me.

Bethesda hadn't been so lucky.

CHAPTER 21

When I woke up, I was in the hospital.

I tried to look around, but my ribs as well as my other wounds were killing me, and I winced in pain at the discovery that I was still alive.

I really didn't mind the agony.

After all, it proved that I'd somehow managed to survive a killer one more time.

I was not surprised to find that Jake was holding my hand the entire time, and he squeezed it tightly as I turned my head gently. "There you are," he said as he kissed my brow. "You've had yourself quite the day, haven't you?"

"I'm so sorry," I said as my words came out in sobs.

"Hey. It's okay. You're alive, Suzanne. That's all that matters."

"I shouldn't have gone out there without you," I said. "It almost cost me my life."

"Stop beating yourself up about it," he said softly. "You're okay."

"How's Bethesda?" I asked him, reliving the sight of her crumpled body lying on the ground.

Jake just shook his head. "She didn't make it."

"I'm sorry. I guess I'm sorry. She tried to kill me," I said, falling back into my own thoughts. "How about my Jeep?"

My husband frowned again. "You're going to need a new one.

You bent the frame on it, and there's nothing that can be done about it. Don't worry about the cost, though. Ethan, Phyllis, and Bobby are going to all chip in and buy you a new one."

"Okay. That's nice," I said, feeling dull and listless. Would Bethesda be dead without my interference? Probably not. Would she ever kill again if I hadn't unmasked her? Who could say? But she couldn't get away with murder, even if Jasper hadn't had that long to live anyway. It was a consequence of my actions that had led to her demise, but I felt as though I'd done a service for my friend, and that was really all that mattered at the moment.

"You're going to actually accept it?" Jake asked, clearly surprised by my decision about getting a new Jeep.

"Why not? I'm not thinking of it as their money. The way I look at it, Jasper is thanking me for finding his killer, and I can live with that."

"I'll let them know," he said. "Listen, we only have a minute before a crowd rushes in here and takes you away from me."

"Are they going to operate? How bad is it?" I asked. There wasn't a great deal of dread in the question. I was at the point where no matter what my fate might be from that moment on, I was going to accept it as best I could.

"No, you're going to be fine. The cuts are all superficial, and I'm not saying that the bruised ribs don't hurt, but at least none of them are broken. They're checking you for a concussion, but that looks good, too. All in all, I'd say you were lucky this time."

Funny, but I didn't feel so lucky.

"Luckier than Jasper or Bethesda, at any rate," I said. "If they aren't taking me to surgery, then who's coming?"

"Who's not?" Jake asked me with a smile. "To start with, your mother and Phillip are nearly here. Grace and Chief Grant are right behind them, and the entire Blake family is coming, too. This is going to be some kind of party."

"Well, it surely beats a wake, doesn't it?" I asked as I winced a little again from the pain.

"Just before you woke up, the nurse told me that you could have something more for the discomfort. It might knock you out, though."

"Let's hold off then, at least for now," I said.

"Listen, you don't have to act tough for me. I know you're strong."

"It's not that," I said. "I just want to be fully aware when everybody comes in. If they give me drugs, I might miss it, and that's something I'm not willing to do."

"I love you, Suzanne," Jake said as he kissed me gently again.

"I love you, too," I answered, just as the crowd of people, each of whom I loved beyond belief, came streaming in.

I'd nearly lost everything that I held dear, so I was going to embrace this time now, no matter how much incidental pain I might feel.

My heart felt just fine—perfect, actually—and in the end, that was all that really mattered to me.

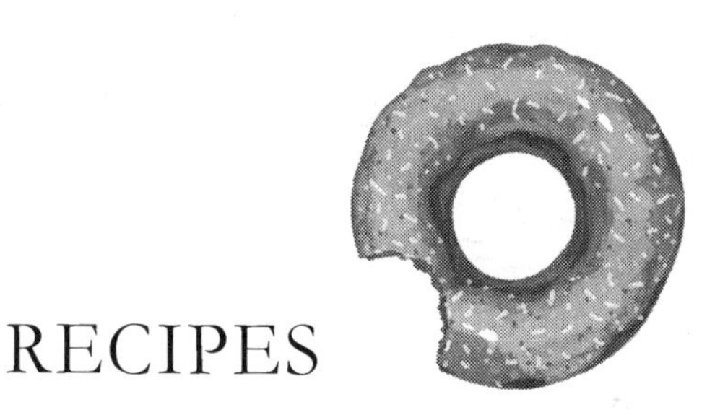

RECIPES

Cranberry Delights

Just like Jasper in the book, my family loves cranberry donuts. There's something about the combination of donuts and berries that is a real treat. The only problem is that sometimes I don't have the time or the energy to make up a fresh batch of donuts from scratch. That's when I turn to a muffin mix, already in a packet and almost ready to go into the fryer or the oven. If you're a hardcore donut maker, I urge you to give these a try anyway. They are true delights to eat, as well as to share.

Ingredients

- 1 package premixed cranberry muffin mix (approx. 7 ounces)
- 3/4 cup unbleached flour
- 1 egg, beaten
- 3/4 cup buttermilk (1% or 2% milk can be substituted)
- Dried cranberries (optional, and certainly not required, but they make a nice addition to the dehydrated berries already in the mix).

Directions

Heat enough canola oil in a large container to 360 degrees F in order to fry the donuts. While waiting for the oil to reach its proper temperature, place the muffin mix in a medium-sized bowl. Then add 1/2 of the flour to the mix, the beaten egg, and the buttermilk. Stir everything together until the dry ingredients are all absorbed into the liquid, but don't overstir the mix. If you're adding cranberries, coat them with the remaining flour and add them now as well. If you're not, add the flour on its own, but remember, don't overstir.

Once the oil is heated to temperature, drop in teaspoon-sized bits of batter. Once they brown on one side, approximately two minutes, flip them over with a long chopstick or other utensil, then remove them from the oil, drain them on paper towels, and then add powdered sugar if desired. If you want to go all out, make up the simple icing listed below and coat them while they are still warm.

Makes 12 to 14 donut rounds

Cranberry Oatmeal Donuts

At my house, we love cranberries in baked goods, whether it is in donuts, bread, or muffins. Lately I've been using dried cranberries in place of raisins with excellent results. So I can feel good about feeding my clan donuts, I also add some oatmeal into the mix so at least it has some semblance of something healthy in it! These donuts are real comfort food to me, and I make them whenever I've had a particularly stressful day.

Ingredients

- 1 egg, beaten
- 1/2 cup sugar (plain granulated white is best)
- 1/2 cup milk (2% or whole milk will do, and if you're desperate, go with 1%)
- 2 tablespoons canola, or any vegetable, oil
- 1 teaspoon vanilla
- 1 cup all-purpose unbleached flour
- 1 teaspoon baking powder
- 1/2 teaspoon cinnamon
- 1/2 teaspoon baking soda
- 1/4 teaspoon salt
- 2 tablespoons oatmeal (old-fashioned, not quick)
- 2 tablespoons dried cranberries

Directions

Heat enough canola oil in a large pot to 360 degrees. While you are waiting, you have plenty of time to mix the batter.

Take a large bowl and beat the egg, then add the sugar slowly until it's incorporated. Next, add the milk, oil, and vanilla, stirring well as you go. Next, sift in the dry ingredients one at a time, but hold out the oatmeal and cranberries for last. Near the end, add them and stir only until the batter is smooth.

When the oil reaches its proper heat, scoop out a tablespoon of batter and rake it into the fryer with another spoon. If the dough doesn't rise from the bottom soon, gently nudge it with a chopstick, being careful not to splatter the hot oil. After 2 minutes, flip the donut rounds, frying for another minute on the other side.

Makes around 8 small donut rounds.

The Cruelest Cruller Around

Just kidding! These are absolutely delightful! I've long been a fan of the store-bought cruller, but these are fun to make, if not as sweet as you might be used to eating. I recommend these for folks who don't like super-sweet treats. I know there are some of you out there, even though I've never run across one personally!

Enjoy!

Ingredients

- 3 eggs, beaten
- 1/2 cup plain white granulated sugar
- 3 tablespoons salted butter, melted
- 1/4 cup whole milk (2% or even 1% will be fine in a pinch)
- 1 teaspoon baking soda
- 3 cups unbleached flour
- 1 teaspoon nutmeg
- 1 teaspoon cinnamon
- 1 teaspoon cream of tartar

Directions

Heat enough canola oil in a large pot to fry your donuts. I've found that 360 degrees is a good temperature.

While the oil is heating, take a large mixing bowl and beat the eggs together, then add the sugar and butter, incorporating it all into the mix. In a smaller bowl, put in the milk and dissolve the baking soda, then add that to the liquid as well. For the dry ingredients, sift together the flour, nutmeg, cinnamon, and cream of tartar. Add these sifted ingredients to the wet, stirring gently as you work.

Roll the dough out to approximately ¼-inch thickness, cut out the donut rounds, and then immediately fry the rounds as well as the holes for two minutes on one side, one on the other. Drain them on paper towels and eat with a simple sugar glaze or with powdered sugar.

Makes 8 to 10 donuts

A Simple Glaze Good For Any Donut

Here's the easiest recipe I use to make my glaze. Honestly, it couldn't be any simpler. If it's too runny, add more sugar. If it's too dry, add more milk. You might end up with more glaze than you can use that way, but that's never been a problem at my house!

Ingredients

- 1/4 cup powdered confectioner's sugar (powdered sugar also works fine)
- 1 to 2 teaspoons whole milk (2% or 1%)
- 1 teaspoon vanilla extract (use the real thing, not imitation)

Instructions

In a small bowl, add the confectioner's sugar and the vanilla extract. Then add the milk ½ a teaspoon at a time until you have a good consistent blend and the glaze drips lazily off your spoon.

When your donuts are still hot, drizzle as much or as little glaze on top of them as you'd like, and then enjoy!

Makes enough to glaze 6 to 10 donuts, depending upon how generous you are with your glaze!

If you enjoy Jessica Beck Mysteries and you would like to be notified when the next book is being released, please visit our website at jessicabeckmysteries.net for valuable information about Jessica's books, and sign up for her new-releases-only mail blast.

Your email address will not be shared, sold, bartered, traded, broadcast, or disclosed in any way. There will be no spam from us, just a friendly reminder when the latest book is being released, and of course, you can drop out at any time.

OTHER BOOKS BY JESSICA BECK

The Donut Mysteries
Glazed Murder
Fatally Frosted
Sinister Sprinkles
Evil Éclairs
Tragic Toppings
Killer Crullers
Drop Dead Chocolate
Powdered Peril
Illegally Iced
Deadly Donuts
Assault and Batter
Sweet Suspects
Deep Fried Homicide
Custard Crime
Lemon Larceny
Bad Bites
Old Fashioned Crooks
Dangerous Dough
Troubled Treats
Sugar Coated Sins
Criminal Crumbs
Vanilla Vices
Raspberry Revenge
Fugitive Filling
Devil's Food Defense
Pumpkin Pleas
Floured Felonies
Mixed Malice
Tasty Trials
Baked Books
Cranberry Crimes

The Classic Diner Mysteries
A Chili Death
A Deadly Beef
A Killer Cake
A Baked Ham
A Bad Egg
A Real Pickle
A Burned Biscuit

The Ghost Cat Cozy Mysteries
Ghost Cat: Midnight Paws
Ghost Cat 2: Bid for Midnight

The Cast Iron Cooking Mysteries
Cast Iron Will
Cast Iron Conviction
Cast Iron Alibi
Cast Iron Motive
Cast Iron Suspicion

Made in the USA
San Bernardino, CA
06 June 2017